ADVENTURE!

The Most Dangerous Game is an exciting collection of stories of high adventure in distant lands:

THE FROZEN WASTES
OF ALASKA

THE TEEMING JUNGLES
OF SOUTH AMERICA

THE MURKY DEPTHS
OF THE HUDSON RIVER

THE STORM-TOSSED WAVES
OF THE PACIFIC

THE SAVAGE PLAINS
OF INDIA

Here are stories that will excite and thrill you with their power and drive.

THE
MOST
DANGEROUS
GAME

AND OTHER STORIES OF ADVENTURE

by

RICHARD CONNELL

JACK LONDON

JAMES THURBER

RUDYARD KIPLING

and others

A BERKLEY HIGHLAND BOOK
published by
BERKLEY PUBLISHING CORPORATION

"The Most Dangerous Game," by Richard Connell. Copyright 1924, by Richard Connell. Copyright renewed, 1952, by Louise Fox Connell. Reprinted by arrangement with the author's estate.

"Leiningen Versus the Ants" by Carl Stephenson. Copyright, 1938, by Carl Stephenson. Reprinted by arrangement with the author.

"Journalism in Tennessee," from *Sketches, New and Old*, by Mark Twain. Reprinted by permisson of Harper & Brothers.

"Alone in Shark Waters," from *Great Sea Stories of Modern Times*, by John Kruse. Copyright, 1953, by John Kruse. Reprinted by permission of The McBride Company, Inc. This story originally appeared in *Collier's*.

"Rikki-Tikki-Tavi," from *The Jungle Book*, by Rudyard Kipling. Reprinted by permission of Mrs. George Bambridge and Double-day and Company, Inc.

"To Build a Fire," by Jack London. Copyright, 1910, by The Macmillan Company. Reprinted by permission of Irving Shepard, Copyright owner.

"Locomotive 38, the Ojibway," from *My Name Is Aram*, by William Saroyan. Copyright 1937, 1938, 1939, 1940, by William Saroyan. Reprinted by permission of Harcourt, Brace & Company.

"High Air," by Borden Chase. Copyright, 1934, by The Butterick Company. Reprinted by arrangement with the author.

"The Secret Life of Walter Mitty," by James Thurber. Copyright, 1939, by The New Yorker Magazine, Inc. Reprinted by arrangement with the author.

BERKLEY EDITION, JUNE, 1957
BERKLEY HIGHLAND EDITION, NOVEMBER, 1962
(2nd Printing)
3rd Printing, January, 1963
4th Printing, August, 1963
5th Printing, January, 1965
6th Printing, November, 1967
7th Printing, February, 1968
8th Printing, June, 1968
9th Printing, August, 1968
10th Printing, September, 1969
11th Printing, September, 1970

SBN 425-01537-8

BERKLEY HIGHLAND BOOKS are published by
Berkley Publishing Corporation
200 Madison Avenue, New York, N. Y. 10016

BERKLEY HIGHLAND BOOKS ® TM 758,135

Printed in the United States of America

CONTENTS

THE MOST DANGEROUS GAME

by *Richard Connell*

"OFF THERE TO THE RIGHT—somewhere—is a large island," said Whitney. "It's rather a mystery—"

"What island is it?" Rainsford asked.

"The old charts call it 'Ship-Trap Island,'" Whitney replied. "A suggestive name, isn't it? Sailors have a curious dread of the place. I don't know why. Some superstition—"

"Can't see it," Rainsford remarked, trying to peer through the dank tropical night that was palpable as it pressed its thick warm blackness in upon the yacht.

"You've good eyes," said Whitney with a laugh, "and I've seen you pick off a moose moving in the brown fall brush at four hundred yards, but you can't see four miles or so through a moonless Caribbean night."

"Nor four yards," admitted Rainsford. "Ugh! It's like moist velvet."

"It will be light enough in Rio," promised Whitney. "We should make it in a few days. I hope the jaguar guns have come from Purdey's. We should have some good hunting up the Amazon. Great sport, hunting."

"The best sport in the world," agreed Rainsford.

"For the hunter," amended Whitney. "Not for the jaguar."

"Don't talk rot, Whitney," said Rainsford. "You're a big-game hunter, not a philosopher. Who cares how a jaguar feels?"

"Perhaps the jaguar does," observed Whitney.

"Bah! They've no understanding."

"Even so, I rather think they understand one thing at least—fear. The fear of pain and the fear of death."

"Nonsense," laughed Rainsford. "This hot weather is making you soft, Whitney. Be a realist. The world is made up of two classes—the hunters and the hunted. Luckily, you and I are hunters. Do you think we've passed that island yet?"

"I can't tell in the dark. I hope so."

"Why?" asked Rainsford.

"The place has a reputation—a bad one."

"Cannibals?" suggested Rainsford.

"Hardly. Even cannibals wouldn't live in such a God-forsaken place. But it's got into sailor lore, somehow. Didn't you notice that the crew's nerves seem a bit jumpy today?"

"They were a bit strange, now you mention it. Even Captain Nielsen—"

"Yes, even that tough-minded old Swede, who'd go up to the devil himself and ask him for a light. Those fishy blue eyes held a look I never saw there before. All I could get out of him was: 'This place has an evil name among seafaring men, sir.' Then he said to me, very gravely: 'Don't you feel anything?'—as if the air about us was actually poisonous. Now, you mustn't laugh when I tell you this—I did feel something like a sudden chill.

"There was no breeze. The sea was as flat as a plate-glass window. We were drawing near the island then. What I felt was a—a mental chill—a sort of sudden dread."

"Pure imagination," said Rainsford. "One superstitious sailor can taint the whole ship's company with his fear."

"Maybe. But sometimes I think sailors have an extra sense that tells them when they are in danger. Sometimes I think evil is a tangible thing—with wave-lengths, just as sound and light have. An evil place can, so to speak, broadcast vibrations of evil. Anyhow, I'm glad we're getting out of this zone. Well, I think I'll turn in now, Rainsford."

"I'm not sleepy," said Rainsford. "I'm going to smoke another pipe up on the after-deck."

"Good night, then, Rainsford. See you at breakfast."

"Right. Good night, Whitney."

There was no sound in the night as Rainsford sat there but the muffled throb of the engine that drove the yacht swiftly through the darkness, and the swish and ripple of the wash of the propeller.

Rainsford, reclining in a steamer chair, indolently puffed on his favorite brier. The sensuous drowsiness of the night was on him. "It's so dark," he thought, "that I could sleep without closing my eyes; the night would be my eyelids—"

An abrupt sound startled him. Off to the right he heard it, and his ears, expert in such matters, could not be mistaken. Again he heard the sound, and again. Somewhere, off in the blackness, some one had fired a gun three times.

Rainsford sprang up and moved quickly to the rail, mystified. He strained his eys in the direction from which the reports had come, but it was like trying to see through a blanket. He leaped upon the rail and balanced himself there, to get greater elevation; his pipe, striking a rope, was knocked from his mouth. He lunged for it; a short, hoarse cry came from his lips as he realized he had reached too far and had lost his balance. The cry was pinched off short as the blood-warm waters of the Caribbean Sea closed over his head.

He struggled up to the surface and tried to cry out, but the wash from the speeding yacht slapped him in the face and the salt water in his open mouth made him gag and strangle. Desperately he struck out with strong strokes after the receding lights of the yacht, but he stopped before he had swum fifty feet. A certain coolheadedness had come to him; it was not the first time he had been in a tight place. There was a chance that his cries could be heard by someone aboard the yacht, but that chance was slender, and grew more slender as the yacht raced on. He wrestled himself out of his clothes, and shouted with all his power. The lights of the yacht became faint and ever-vanishing fireflies; then they were blotted entirely by the night.

Rainsford remembered the shots. They had come from

the right, and doggedly he swam in that direction, swimming with slow, deliberate strokes, conserving his strength. For a seemingly endless time he fought the sea. He began to count his strokes desperately; he could do possibly a hundred more, and then—

Rainsford heard a sound. It came out of the darkness, a high, screaming sound, the sound of an animal in an extremity of anguish and terror.

He did not recognize the animal that made the sound; he did not try to; with fresh vitality he swam toward the sound. He heard it again; then it was cut short by another noise, crisp, staccato.

"Pistol shot," muttered Rainsford swimming on.

Ten minutes of determined effort brought another sound to his ears—the most welcome he had ever heard —the muttering and growling of the sea breaking on a rocky shore. He was almost on the rocks before he saw them; on a night less calm he would have been shattered against them. With his remaining strength he dragged himself from the swirling waters. Jagged crags appeared to jut up into the opaqueness; he forced himself upward, hand over hand. Gasping, his hands raw, he reached a flat place at the top. Dense jungle came down to the very edge of the cliffs. What perils that tangle of trees and underbrush might hold for him did not concern Rainsford just then. All he knew was that he was safe from his enemy, the sea, and that utter weariness was on him. He flung himself down at the jungle edge and tumbled headlong into the deepest sleep of his life.

When he opened his eyes he knew from the position of the sun that it was late in the afternoon. Sleep had given him new vigor; a sharp hunger was picking at him. He looked about him, almost cheerfully.

"Where there are pistol shots, there are men. Where there are men, there is food," he thought. "But what kind of men?" he wondered, "in so forbidding a place?" An unbroken front of snarled and jagged jungle fringed the shore.

He saw no sign of a trail through the closely knit web of weeds and trees; it was easier to go along the shore, and Rainsford floundered along by the water. Not far from where he had landed, he stopped.

Some wounded thing, by the evidence a large animal, had thrashed about in the underbrush; the jungle weeds were crushed down and the moss was lacerated; one patch of weeds was stained crimson. A small, glittering object not far away caught Rainsford's eye and he picked it up. It was an empty cartridge.

"A twenty-two," he remarked. "That's odd. It must have been a fairly large animal, too. The hunter had his nerve to tackle it with a light gun. It's clear that the brute put up a fight. I suppose the first three shots I heard was when the hunter flushed his quarry and wounded it. The last shot was when he trailed it here and finished it."

He examined the ground closely and found what he had hoped to find—the print of hunting boots. They pointed along the cliff in the direction he had been going. Eagerly he hurried along, now slipping on a rotten log or a loose stone, but making headway; night was beginning to settle down on the island.

Bleak darkness was blacking out the sea and jungle when Rainsford sighted the lights. He came upon them as he turned a crook in the coast line, and his first thought was that he had come upon a village, for there were so many lights. But as he forged along he saw to his great astonishment that all the lights were in one enormous building—a lofty structure with pointed towers plunging upward into the gloom. His eyes made out the shadowy outlines of a palatial château; it was set on a high bluff, and on three sides of it cliffs dived down to where the sea licked greedy lips in the shadows.

"Mirage," thought Rainsford. But it was no mirage, he found, when he opened the tall spiked gate. The stone steps were real enough; the massive door with a leering gargoyle for a knocker was real enough; yet about it all hung an air of unreality.

He lifted the knocker, and it creaked up stiffly, as if it had never before been used. He let it fall, and it startled him with its booming loudness. He thought he heard footsteps within; the door remained closed. Again Rainsford

lifted the heavy knocker, and let it fall. The door opened
then, opened as suddenly as if it were on a spring, and
Rainsford stood blinking in the river of glaring gold light
that poured out. The first thing Rainsford's eyes dis-
cerned was the largest man he had ever seen—a gigantic
creature, solidly made and black-bearded to the waist. In
his hand the man held a long-barrel-revolver, and he was
pointing it straight at Rainsford's heart.

Out of the snarl of beard two small eyes regarded
Rainsford.

"Don't be alarmed," said Rainsford, with a smile
which he hoped was disarming. "I'm no robber. I fell off
a yacht. My name is Sanger Rainsford of New York
City."

The menacing look in the eyes did not change. The revolver pointed as rigidly as if the giant were a statue. He
gave no sign that he understood Rainsford's words, or
that he had even heard them. He was dressed in uniform,
a black uniform trimmed with grey astrakhan.

"I'm Sanger Rainsford of New York," Rainsford began
again. "I fell off a yacht. I am hungry."

The man's only answer was to raise with his thumb the
hammer of his revolver. Then Rainsford saw the man's
free hand go to his forehead in a military salute, and he
saw him click his heels together and stand at attention.
Another man was coming down the broad marble steps,
an erect, slender man in evening clothes. He advanced to
Rainsford and held out his hand.

In a cultivated voice marked by a slight accent that
gave it added precision and deliberateness, he said: "It is
a very great pleasure and honor to welcome Mr. Sanger
Rainsford, the celebrated hunter, to my home."

Automatically Rainsford shook the man's hand.

"I've read your book about hunting snow leopards in
Tibet, you see," explained the man. "I am General
Zaroff."

Rainsford's first impression was that the man was sin-
gularly handsome; his second was that there was an original, almost bizarre quality about the general's face. He
was a tall man past middle age, for his hair was a vivid

white; but his thick eyebrows and pointed military mustache were as black as the night from which Rainsford had come. His eyes, too, were black and very bright. He had high cheek bones, a sharp-cut nose, a spare, dark face, the face of a man used to giving orders, the face of an aristocrat. Turning to the giant in uniform, the general made a sign. The giant put away his pistol, saluted, withdrew.

"Ivan is an incredibly strong fellow," remarked the general, "but he has the misfortune to be deaf and dumb. A simple fellow, but, I'm afraid, like all his race, a bit savage."

"Is he Russian?"

"He is a Cossack," said the general, and his smile showed red lips and pointed teeth. "So am I. . . . Come," he said, "we shouldn't be chatting here. We can talk later. Now you want clothes, food, rest. You shall have them. This is a most restful spot."

Ivan had reappeared, and the general spoke to him with lips that moved but gave forth no sound.

"Follow Ivan, if you please, Mr. Rainsford," said the general. "I was about to have my dinner when you came. I'll wait for you. You'll find that my clothes will fit you, I think."

It was to a huge, beam-ceilinged bedroom with a canopied bed big enough for six men that Rainsford followed the silent giant. Ivan laid out an evening suit, and Rainsford, as he put it on, noticed that it came from a London tailor who ordinarily cut and sewed for none below the rank of duke.

The dining-room to which Ivan conducted him was in many ways remarkable. There was a medieval magnificence about it; it suggested a baronial hall of feudal times with its oaken panels, its high ceiling, its vast refectory table where two-score men could sit down to eat. About the hall were the mounted heads of many animals—lions, tigers, elephants, moose, bears; larger or more perfect specimens Rainsford had never seen. At the great table the general was sitting, alone.

"You'll have a cocktail, Mr. Rainsford," he suggested.

The cocktail was surpassingly good; and Rainsford noted, the table appointments were of the finest,—the linen, the crystal, the silver, the china.

They were eating *borsch,* the rich, red soup with whipped cream so dear to Russian palates. Half apologetically General Zaroff said: "We do our best to preserve the amenities of civilization here. Please forgive any lapses. We are well off the beaten track, you know. Do you think the champagne has suffered from its long ocean trip?"

"Not in the least," declared Rainsford. He was finding the general a most thoughtful and affable host, a true cosmopolite. But there was one small trait of the general's that made Rainsford uncomfortable. Whenever he looked up from his plate he found the general studying him, appraising him narrowly.

"Perhaps," said General Zaroff, "you were surprised that I recognized your name. You see, I read all books on hunting, published in English, French, and Russian. I have but one passion in my life, Mr. Rainsford, and it is the hunt."

"You have some wonderful heads here," said Rainsford as he ate a particularly well cooked filet mignon. "That Cape buffalo is the largest I ever saw."

"Oh, that fellow. Yes, he was a monster."

"Did he charge you?"

"Hurled me against a tree," said the general. "Fractured my skull. But I got the brute."

"I've always thought," said Rainsford, "that the Cape buffalo is the most dangerous of all big game."

For a moment the general did not reply; he was smiling his curious red-lipped smile. Then he said slowly: "No. You are wrong, sir. The Cape buffalo is not the most dangerous big game." He sipped his wine. "Here in my preserve on this island," he said in the same slow tone, "I hunt more dangerous game."

Rainsford expressed his surprise. "Is there big game on this island?"

The general nodded. "The biggest."

"Really?"

"Oh, it isn't here naturally, of course. I have to stock the island."

"What have you imported, general?" Rainsford asked. "Tigers?"

The general smiled. "No," he said. "Hunting tigers ceased to interest me some years ago. I exhausted their possibilities, you see. No thrill left in tigers, no real danger. I live for danger, Mr. Rainsford."

The general took from his pocket a gold cigarette case and offered his guest a long black cigarette with a silver tip; it was perfumed and gave off a smell like incense.

"We will have some capital hunting, you and I," said the general. "I shall be most glad to have your society."

"But what game—" began Rainsford.

"I'll tell you," said the general. "You will be amused, I know. I think I may say, in all modesty, that I have done a rare thing. I have invented a new sensation. May I pour you another glass of port, Mr. Rainsford?"

"Thank you, general."

The general filled both glasses, and said: "God makes some men poets. Some He makes kings, some beggars. Me He made a hunter. My hand was made for the trigger, my father said. He was a very rich man with a quarter of a million acres in the Crimea, and he was an ardent sportsman. When I was only five years old he gave me a little gun, specially made in Moscow for me, to shoot sparrows with. When I shot some of his prize turkeys with it, he did not punish me; he complimented me on my marksmanship. I killed my first bear in the Caucasus when I was ten. My whole life has been one prolonged hunt. I went into the army—it was expected of noblemen's sons—and for a time commanded a division of Cossack cavalry, but my real interest was always the hunt. I have hunted every kind of game in every land. It would be impossible for me to tell you how many animals I have killed."

The general puffed at his cigarette.

"After the debacle in Russia I left the country, for it was imprudent for an officer of the Czar to stay there. Many noble Russians lost everything. I, luckily, had invested heavily in American securities, so I shall never have to open a tea-room in Monte Carlo or drive a taxi in Paris. Naturally, I continued to hunt—grizzlies in your Rockies, crocodiles in the Ganges, rhinoceroses in East Africa. It was in Africa that the Cape buffalo hit me and laid me up for six months. As soon as I recovered I started for the Amazon to hunt jaguars, for I had heard they were unusually cunning. They weren't." The Cossack sighed. "They were no match at all for a hunter with his wits about him, and a high-powered rifle. I was bitterly disappointed. I was lying in my tent with a splitting headache one night when a terrible thought pushed its way into my mind. Hunting was beginning to bore me. And hunting, remember, had been my life. I have heard that in America business men often go to pieces when they give up the business that has been their life."

"Yes, that's so," said Rainsford.

The general smiled. "I had no wish to go to pieces," he said. "I must do something. Now, mine is an analytical mind, Mr. Rainsford. Doubtless that is why I enjoy the problems of the chase."

"No doubt, General Zaroff."

"So," continued the general, "I asked myself why the hunt no longer fascinated me. You are much younger than I am, Mr. Rainsford, and have not hunted as much, but you perhaps can guess the answer."

"What was it?"

"Simply this: hunting had ceased to be what you call 'a sporting proposition.' It had become too easy. I always got my quarry. Always. There is no greater bore than perfection."

The general lit a fresh cigarette.

"No animal had a chance with me any more. That is no boast; it is a mathematical certainty. The animal had nothing but his legs and his instinct. Instinct is no match for reason. When I thought of this it was a tragic moment for me, I can tell you."

Rainsford leaned across the table, absorbed in what his host was saying.

"It came to me as an inspiration what I must do," the general went on.

"And that was?"

The general smiled the quiet smile of one who has faced an obstacle and surmounted it with success. "I had to invent a new animal to hunt," he said.

"A new animal? You are joking."

"Not at all," said the general. "I never joke about hunting. I needed a new animal. I found one. So I bought this island, built this house, and here I do my hunting. The island is perfect for my purposes—there are jungles with a maze of trails in them, hills, swamps—"

"But the animal, General Zaroff?"

"Oh," said the general, "it supplies me with the most exciting hunting in the world. No other hunting compares with it for an instant. Every day I hunt, and I never grow bored now, for I have a quarry with which I can match my wits."

Rainsford's bewilderment showed in his face.

"I wanted the ideal animal to hunt," explained the general. "So I said: 'What are the attributes of an ideal quarry?' And the answer was, of course: 'It must have courage, cunning, and, above all, it must be able to reason.' "

"But no animal can reason," objected Rainsford.

"My dear fellow," said the general, "there is one that can."

"But you can't mean—" gasped Rainsford.

"And why not?"

"I can't believe you are serious, General Zaroff. This is a grisly joke."

"Why should I not be serious? I am speaking of hunting."

"Hunting? Good heavens, General Zaroff, what you speak of is murder."

The general laughed with entire good nature. He regarded Rainsford quizzically. "I refuse to believe that so modern and civilized a young man as you seem to be harbors romantic ideas about the values of human life. Surely your experiences in the war—" He stopped.

"Did not make me condone cold-blooded murder," finished Rainsford stiffly.

Laughter shook the general. "How extraordinarily droll you are!" he said. "One does not expect nowadays to find a young man of the educated class, even in America, with such a naïve, and, if I may say so, mid-Victorian point of view. It's like finding a snuff-box in a limousine. Ah, well, doubtless you had Puritan ancestors. So many Americans appear to have had. I'll wager you'll forget your notions when you go hunting with me. You've a genuine new thrill in store for you, Mr. Rainsford."

"Thank you, I'm a hunter, not a murderer."

"Dear me," said the general, quite unruffled, "again that unpleasant word. But I think I can show you that your scruples are quite ill founded."

"Yes?"

"Life is for the strong, to be lived by the strong, and, if need be, taken by the strong. The weak of the world were put here to give the strong pleasure. I am strong. Why should I not use my gift? If I wish to hunt, why should I not? I hunt the scum of the earth—sailors from tramp ships—lascars, blacks, Chinese, whites, mongrels—a thoroughbred horse or hound is worth more than a score of them."

"But they are men," said Rainsford hotly.

"Precisely," said the general. "That is why I use them. It gives me pleasure. They can reason, after a fashion. So they are dangerous."

"But where do you get them?"

The general's left eyelid fluttered down in a wink. "This island is called Ship-Trap," he answered. "Sometimes an angry god of the high seas sends them to me. Sometimes, when Providence is not so kind, I help Providence a bit. Come to the window with me."

Rainsford went to the window, and looked out toward the sea.

"Watch! Out there!" exclaimed the general, pointing into the night. Rainsford's eyes saw only blackness, and then, as the general pressed a button, far out to sea Rainsford saw the flash of lights.

The general chuckled. "They indicate a channel," he said, "where there's none: giant rocks with razor edges crouch like a sea monster with wide-open jaws. They can crush a ship as easily as I crush this nut." He dropped a walnut on the hardwood floor and brought his heel grinding down on it. "Oh, yes," he said casually, as if in answer to a question, "I have electricity. We try to be civilized here."

"Civilized? And you shoot down men?"

A trace of anger was in the general's black eyes, but it was there for but a second, and he said, in his most pleasant manner: "Dear me, what a righteous young man you are! I assure you I do not do the thing you suggest. That would be barbarous. I treat these visitors with every consideration. They get plenty of good food and exercise. They get into splendid physical condition. You shall see for yourself to-morrow."

"What do you mean?"

"We'll visit my training school," smiled the general, "It's in the cellar. I have about a dozen pupils down there now. They're from the Spanish bark *San Lucar,* that had the bad luck to go on the rocks out there. A very inferior lot, I regret to say. Poor specimens, and more accustomed to the deck than to the jungle."

He raised his hand and Ivan, who served as waiter, brought thick Turkish coffee. Rainsford, with an effort, held his tongue in check.

"It's a game, you see," pursued the general blandly. "I suggest to one of them that we go hunting. I give him a supply of food and an excellent hunting knife. I give him three hours' start. I am to follow, armed only with a pistol of the smallest calibre and range. If my quarry eludes me for three whole days, he wins the game. If I find him"—the general smiled—"he loses."

"Suppose he refuses to be hunted?"

"Oh," said the general, "I give him his option, of course. He need not play that game if he doesn't wish to. If he does not wish to hunt, I turn him over to Ivan. Ivan once had the honor of serving as official knouter to the Great White Czar, and he has his own ideas of sport. Invariably, Mr. Rainsford, invariably they choose the hunt."

"And if they win?"

The smile on the general's face widened. "To date I have not lost," he said.

Then he added, hastily, "I don't wish you to think me a braggart, Mr. Rainsford. Many of them afford only the most elementary sort of problem. Occasionally I strike a tartar. One almost did win. I eventually had to use the dogs."

"The dogs?"

"This way, please. I'll show you."

The general steered Rainsford to a window. The lights from the windows sent a flickering illumination that made grotesque patterns on the courtyard below, and Rainsford could see moving about there a dozen or so huge black shapes; as they turned toward him, their eyes glittered greenly.

"A rather good lot, I think," observed the general. "They are let out at seven every night. If anyone should try to get into my house—or out of it—something extremely regrettable would occur to him." He hummed a snatch of song from the Folies-Bergères.

"And now," said the general, "I want to show you my new collection of heads. Will you come with me to the library?"

"I hope," said Rainsford, "that you will excuse me tonight, General Zaroff. I'm really not feeling at all well."

"Ah, indeed?" the general inquired solicitously. "Well, I suppose that's only natural, after your long swim. You need a good, restful night's sleep. Tomorrow you'll feel like a new man, I'll wager. Then we'll hunt, eh? I've one rather promising prospect—"

Rainsford was hurrying from the room.

"Sorry you can't go with me tonight," called the general. "I expect rather fair sport—a big, strong black. He looks resourceful—Well, good night, Mr. Rainsford; I hope that you have a good night's rest."

The bed was good and the pajamas of the softest silk, and he was tired in every fiber of his being, but nevertheless Rainsford could not quiet his brain with the opiate of

sl   ves wide open. Once he thought he heard
st   ide his room. He sought to throw open
t   open. He went to the window and
l   vas high up in one of the towers.
            au were out now, and it was dark
            vas a fragment of sallow moon, and
            ould see, dimly, the courtyard; there,
            in the pattern of shadow, were black,
            e hounds heard him at the window and
            tantly, with their green eyes. Rainsford
            bed and lay down. By many methods he
            put himself to sleep. He had achieved a doze
      en, just as morning began to come, he heard, far off in
the jungle, the faint report of a pistol.

General Zaroff did not appear until luncheon. He was
dressed faultlessly in the tweeds of a country squire. He
was solicitous about the state of Rainsford's health.

"As for me," sighed the general, "I do not feel so well.
I am worried, Mr. Rainsford. Last night I detected traces
of my old complaint."

To Rainsford's questioning glance the general said:
"Ennui. Boredom."

Then, taking a second helping of crêpes suzette, the
general explained: "The hunting was not good last night.
The fellow lost his head. He made a straight trail that
offered no problems at all. That's the trouble with these
sailors; they have dull brains to begin with, and they do
not know how to get about in the woods. They do exces-
sively stupid and obvious things. It's most annoying. Will
you have another glass of Chablis, Mr. Rainsford?"

"General," said Rainsford firmly, "I wish to leave this
island at once."

The general raised his thickets of eyebrows; he seemed
hurt. "But, my dear fellow," the general protested,
"you've only just come. You've had no hunting—"

"I wish to go today," said Rainsford. He saw the dead
black eyes of the general on him, studying him. General
Zaroff's face suddenly brightened.

He filled Rainsford's glass with venerable Chablis from a dusty bottle.

"Tonight," said the general, "we will hunt—you and I."

Rainsford shook his head. "No, general," he said. "I will not hunt."

The general shrugged his shoulders and delicately ate a hothouse grape. "As you wish, my friend," he said. "The choice rests entirely with you. But may I not venture to suggest that you will find my idea of sport more diverting than Ivan's?"

He nodded toward the corner to where the giant stood, scowling, his thick arms crossed on his hogshead of chest.

"You don't mean—" cried Rainsford.

"My dear fellow," said the general, "have I not told you I always mean what I say about hunting? This is really an inspiration. I drink to a foeman worthy of my steel —at last."

The general raised his glass, but Rainsford sat staring at him.

"You'll find this game worth playing," the general said enthusiastically. "Your brain against mine. Your wood-craft against mine. Outdoor chess! And the stake is not without value, eh?"

"And if I win—" began Rainsford huskily.

"I'll cheerfully acknowledge myself defeated if I do not find you by midnight of the third day," said General Zaroff. "My sloop will place you on the mainland near a town."

The general read what Rainsford was thinking.

"Oh, you can trust me," said the Cossack. "I will give you my word as a gentleman and a sportsman. Of course you, in turn, must agree to say nothing of your visit here."

"I'll agree to nothing of the kind," said Rainsford.

"Oh," said the general, "in that case— But why dis-cuss it now? Three days hence we can discuss it over a bottle of Veuve Cliquot, unless—"

The general sipped his wine.

Then a businesslike air animated him. "Ivan," he said to Rainsford, "will supply you with hunting clothes, food, a knife. I suggest you wear moccasins; they leave a poorer trail. I suggest too that you avoid the big swamp in the southeast corner of the island. We call it Death Swamp. There's quicksand there. One foolish fellow tried it. The deplorable part of it was that Lazarus followed him. You can imagine my feelings, Mr. Rainsford. I loved Lazarus; he was the finest hound in my pack. Well, I must beg you to excuse me now. I always take a siesta after lunch. You'll want to start, no doubt. I shall not follow till dusk. Hunting at night is so much more exciting than by day, don't you think? Au revoir, Mr. Rainsford, au revoir."

General Zaroff, with a deep courtly bow, strolled from the room.

From another room came Ivan. Under one arm he carried khaki hunting clothes, a haversack of food, a leather sheath containing a long-bladed hunting knife; his right hand rested on a cocked revolver thrust in the crimson sash about his waist. . . .

Rainsford had fought his way through the bush for two hours. "I must keep my nerve. I must keep my nerve," he said through tight teeth.

He had not been entirely clear-headed when the château gates snapped shut behind him. His whole idea at first was to put distance between himself and General Zaroff, and, to this end, he had plunged along, spurred on by the sharp rowels of something very like panic. Now he had got a grip on himself, had stopped, and was taking stock of himself and the situation.

He saw that straight flight was futile; inevitably it would bring him face to face with the sea. He was in a picture with a frame of water, and his operations, clearly, must take place within that frame.

"I'll give him a trail to follow," muttered Rainsford, and he struck off from the rude path he had been following into the trackless wilderness. He executed a series of intricate loops; he doubled on his trail again and again, recalling all the lore of the fox hunt, and all the dodges of the fox. Night found him leg-weary, with hands and face lashed by the branches, on a thickly wooded ridge. He

knew it would be insane to blunder on through the dark,
even if he had the strength. His need for rest was imperative and he thought: "I have played the fox, now I must
play the cat of the fable." A big tree with a thick trunk
and outspread branches was near by, and, taking care to
leave not the slightest mark, he climbed up into the
crotch, and stretching out on one of the broad limbs,
after a fashion, rested. Rest brought him new confidence
and almost a feeling of security. Even so zealous a hunter
as General Zaroff could not trace him there, he told himself; only the devil himself could follow that complicated
trail through the jungle after dark. But, perhaps, the general was a devil—

An apprehensive night crawled slowly by like a wounded snake, and sleep did not visit Rainsford, although the
silence of a dead world was on the jungle. Toward morning when a dingy gray was varnishing the sky, the cry of
some startled bird focussed Rainsford's attention in that
direction. Something was coming through the bush, coming slowly, carefully, coming by the same winding way
Rainsford had come. He flattened himself down on the
limb, and through a screen of leaves almost as thick as
tapestry, he watched. The thing that was approaching him
was a man.

It was General Zaroff. He made his way along with his
eyes fixed in utmost concentration on the ground before
him. He paused, almost beneath the tree, dropped to his
knees and studied the ground. Rainsford's impulse was to
hurl himself down like a panther, but he saw that the
general's right hand held something small and metallic—
an automatic pistol.

The hunter shook his head several times, as if he were
puzzled. Then he straightened up and took from his case
one of his black cigarettes; its pungent incenselike smoke
floated up to Rainsford's nostrils. Rainsford held his
breath. The general's eyes had left the ground and were
traveling inch by inch up the tree. Rainsford froze there,
every muscle tensed for a spring. But the sharp eyes of
the hunter stopped before they reached the limb where
Rainsford lay; a smile spread over his brown face. Very

deliberately he blew a smoke ring into the air; then he turned his back on the tree and walked carelessly away, back along the trail he had come. The swish of the underbrush against his hunting boots grew fainter and fainter.

The pent-up air burst hotly from Rainsford's lungs. His first thought made him feel sick and numb. The general could follow a trail through the woods at night; he could follow an extremely difficult trail; he must have uncanny powers; only by the merest chance had the Cossack failed to see his quarry.

Rainsford's second thought was even more terrible. It sent a shudder of cold horror through his whole being. Why had the general smiled? Why had he turned back?

Rainsford did not want to believe what his reason told him was true, but the truth was as evident as the sun that had by now pushed through the morning mists. The general was playing with him! The general was saving him for another day's sport! The Cossack was the cat; he was the mouse. Then it was that Rainsford knew the full meaning of terror.

"I will not lose my nerve. I will not."

He slid down from the tree, and struck off again into the woods. His face was set and he forced the machinery of his mind to function. Three hundred yards from his hiding place he stopped where a huge dead tree leaned precariously on a smaller, living one. Throwing off his sack of food, Rainsford took his knife from its sheath and began to work with all his energy.

The job was finished at last, and he threw himself down behind a fallen log a hundred feet away. He did not have to wait long. The cat was coming again to play with the mouse.

Following the trail with the sureness of a blood-hound, came General Zaroff. Nothing escaped those searching black eyes, no crushed blade of grass, no bent twig, no mark, no matter how faint, in the moss. So intent was the Cossack on his stalking that he was upon the thing Rainsford had made before he saw it. His foot touched the protruding bough that was the trigger. Even as he touched it, the general sensed his danger and leaped back with the agility of an ape. But he was not quite quick enough; the dead tree, delicately adjusted to rest on the cut living one, crashed down and struck the general a glancing blow on the shoulder as it fell; but for his alertness, he must have been smashed beneath it. He staggered, but he did not fall; not did he drop his revolver. He stood there, rubbing his injured shoulder, and Rainsford, with fear again gripping his heart, heard the general's mocking laugh ring through the jungle.

"Rainsford," called the general, "if you are within sound of my voice, as I suppose you are, let me congratulate you. Not many men know how to make a Malay man-catcher. Luckily for me, I too have hunted in Malacca. You are proving interesting, Mr. Rainsford. I am going now to have my wound dressed; it's only a slight one. But I shall be back. I shall be back."

When the general, nursing his bruised shoulder, had gone, Rainsford took up his flight again. It was flight now, a desperate, hopeless flight, that carried him on for some hours. Dusk came, then darkness, and still he pressed on. The ground grew softer under his moccasins; the vegetation grew ranker, denser; insects bit him savagely. Then, as he stepped forward, his foot sank into the ooze. He tried to wrench it back, but the muck sucked viciously at his foot as if it were a giant leech. With a violent effort, he tore his foot loose. He knew where he was now. Death Swamp and its quicksand.

His hands were tight closed as if his nerve were something tangible that someone in the darkness was trying to tear from his grip. The softness of the earth had given him an idea. He stepped back from the quicksand a dozen feet or so and, like some huge prehistoric beaver, he began to dig.

Rainsford had dug himself in in France when a second's delay meant death. That had been a placid pastime compared to his digging now. The pit grew deeper; when it was above his shoulders, he climbed out and from some hard saplings cut stakes and sharpened them to a fine point. These stakes he planted in the bottom of the pit with the point sticking up. With flying fingers he wove a rough carpet of weeds and branches and with it he covered the mouth of the pit. Then, wet with sweat and aching with tiredness, he crouched behind the stump of a lightning-charred tree.

He knew his pursuer was coming; he heard the padding sound of feet on the soft earth, and the night breeze brought him the perfume of the general's cigarette. It seemed to Rainsford that the general was coming with unusual swiftness; he was not feeling his way along, foot by foot. Rainsford, crouching there, could not see the general, nor could he see the pit. He lived a year in a minute. Then he felt an impulse to cry aloud with joy, for he heard the sharp crackle of the breaking branches as the cover of the pit gave way; he heard the sharp scream of pain as the pointed stakes found their mark. He leaped up from his place of concealment. Then he cowered back. Three feet from the pit a man was standing, with an electric torch in his hand.

"You've done well, Rainsford," the voice of the general called. "Your Burmese tiger pit has claimed one of my best dogs. Again you score. Again you score. I think, Mr. Rainsford, I'll see what you can do against my whole pack. I'm going home for a rest now. Thank you for a most amusing evening."

At daybreak Rainsford, lying near the swamp, was awakened by a sound that made him know that he had new things to learn about fear. It was a distant sound, faint and wavering, but he knew it. It was the baying of a pack of hounds.

Rainsford knew he could do one of two things. He could stay where he was and wait. That was suicide. He could flee. That was postponing the inevitable. For a moment he stood there, thinking. An idea that held a wild chance came to him, and tightening his belt, he headed from the swamp.

The baying of the hounds drew nearer, then still nearer, even nearer. On a ridge Rainsford climbed a tree. Down a watercourse, not a quarter of a mile away, he could see the bush moving. Straining his eyes, he saw the lean figure of General Zaroff; just ahead of him Rainsford

made out another figure whose wide shoulders surged
through the tall jungle weeds; it was the giant Ivan, and
he seemed pulled forward by some unseen force; Rainsford knew that Ivan must be holding the pack in leash.

They would be on him any minute now. His mind
worked frantically. He thought of a native trick he had
learned in Uganda. He slid down the tree. He caught hold
of a springy young sapling and to it he fastened his hunting knife, with the blade pointing down the trail; with a
bit of wild grapevine he tied back the sapling. Then he
ran for his life. The hounds raised their voices as they hit
the fresh scent. Rainsford knew now how an animal at
bay feels.

He had to stop to get his breath. The baying of the
hounds stopped abruptly, and Rainsford's heart stopped
too. They must have reached the knife.

He shinned excitedly up a tree and looked back. His
pursuers had stopped. But the hope that was in Rainsford's brain when he climbed died, for he saw in the shal-
low valley that General Zaroff was still on his feet. But
Ivan was not. The knife, driven by the recoil of the
springing tree, had not wholly failed.

Rainsford had hardly tumbled to the ground when the
pack took up the cry again.

"Nerve, nerve, nerve!" he panted as he dashed along.
A blue gap showed between the trees dead ahead. Even
nearer drew the hounds. Rainsford forced himself on toward the gap. He reached it. It was the shore of the sea.
Across a cove he could see the gloomy gray stone of the
château. Twenty feet below him the sea rumbled and
hissed. Rainsford hesitated. He heard the hounds. Then
he leaped far out into the sea. . . .

When the general and his pack reached the place by
the sea, the Cossack stopped. For some minutes he stood
regarding the blue-green expanse of water. He shrugged
his shoulders. Then he sat down, took a drink of brandy
from a silver flask, lit a perfumed cigarette, and hummed
a bit from *Madame Butterfly*.

General Zaroff had an exceedingly good dinner in his
great paneled dining-hall that evening. With it he had a

bottle of Pol Roger and half a bottle of Chambertin. Two slight annoyances kept him from perfect enjoyment. One was the thought that it would be difficult to replace Ivan; the other was that his quarry had escaped him; of course the American hadn't played the game—so thought the general as he tasted his after-dinner liqueur. In his library he read, to sooth himself, from the works of Marcus Aurelius. At ten he went up to his bedroom. He was deliciously tired, he said to himself, as he locked himself in. There was a little moonlight, so, before turning on his light, he went to the window and looked down at the courtyard. He could see the great hounds, and he called "Better luck another time" to them. He switched on the light.

A man, who had been hiding in the curtains of the bed, was standing there.

"Rainsford!" screamed the general. "How in heaven's name did you get here?"

"Swam," said Rainsford. "I found it quicker than walking through the jungle."

The general sucked in his breath and smiled. "I congratulate you," he said. "You have won the game."

Rainsford did not smile. "I am still a beast at bay," he said in a low, hoarse voice. "Get ready, General Zaroff."

The general made one of his deepest bows. "I see," he said. "Splendid! One of us is to furnish a repast for the hounds. The other will sleep in this very excellent bed. On guard, Rainsford." . . .

He had never slept in a better bed, Rainsford decided.

LEININGEN VERSUS THE ANTS

by Carl Stephenson

"UNLESS THEY ALTER their course and there's no reason why they should, they'll reach your plantation in two days at the latest."

Leningen sucked placidly at a cigar about the size of a corn cob and for a few seconds gazed without answering at the agitated District Commissioner. Then he took the cigar from his lips, and leaned slightly forward. With his bristling grey hair, bulky nose, and lucid eyes, he had the look of an aging and shabby eagle.

"Decent of you," he murmured, "paddling all this way just to give me the tip. But you're pulling my leg of course when you say I must do a bunk. Why, even a herd of saurians couldn't drive me from this plantation of mine."

The Brazilian official threw up lean and lanky arms and clawed the air with wildly distended fingers. "Leiningen!" he shouted. "You're insane! They're not creatures you can fight—they're an elemental—an 'act of God!' Ten miles long, two miles wide—ants, nothing but ants! And every single one of them a fiend from hell; before you can spit three times they'll eat a full-grown buffalo to the bones. I tell you if you don't clear out at once there'll be nothing left of you but a skeleton picked as clean as your plantation."

Leiningen grinned. "Act of God, my eye! Anyway, I'm not an old woman; I'm not going to run for it just because an elemental's on the way. And don't think I'm the kind of fathead who tries to fend off lightning with his fists, either. I use my intelligence, old man. With me, the brain isn't a second blindgut; I know what it's there for. When I began this model farm and plantation three years ago, I took into account all that could conceivably happen to it. And now I'm ready for anything and everything—including your ants."

The Brazilian rose heavily to his feet. "I've done my best," he gasped. "Your obstinacy endangers not only yourself, but the lives of your four hundred workers. You don't know these ants!"

Leiningen accompanied him down to the river, where the Government launch was moored. The vessel cast off. As it moved downstream, the exclamation mark neared the rail and began waving its arms frantically. Long after the launch had disappeared round the bend, Leiningen thought he could still hear that dimming, imploring voice. "You don't know them, I tell you! *You don't know them!*"

But the reported enemy was by no means unfamiliar to the planter. Before he started work on his settlement, he had lived long enough in the country to see for himself the fearful devastations sometimes wrought by these ravenous insects in their campaigns for food. But since then he had planned measures of defense accordingly, and these, he was convinced, were in every way adequate to withstand the approaching peril.

Moreover, during his three years as a planter, Leiningen had met and defeated drought, flood, plague and all other "acts of God" which had come against him—unlike his fellow-settlers in the district, who had made little or no resistance. This unbroken success he attributed solely to the observance of his lifelong motto: *The human brain needs only to become fully aware of its powers to conquer even the elements.* Dullards reeled senselessly and aimlessly into the abyss; cranks, however brilliant, lost their heads when circumstances suddenly altered or accelerated and ran into stone walls, sluggards drifted with the current until they were caught in whirlpools and dragged under. But such disasters, Leiningen contended, merely strengthened his argument that intelligence, directed aright, invariably makes man the master of his fate.

Yes, Leiningen had always known how to grapple with life. Even here, in this Brazilian wilderness, his brain had triumphed over every difficulty and danger it had so far encountered. First he had vanquished primal forces by cunning and organization, then he had enlisted the resources of modern science to increase miraculously the yield of his plantation. And now he was sure he would prove more than a match for the "irresistible" ants.

That same evening, however, Leiningen assembled his workers. He had no intention of waiting till the news reached their ears from other sources. Most of them had been born in the district; the cry "The ants are coming!" was to them an imperative signal for instant, panic-stricken flight, a spring for life itself. But so great was the Indian's trust in Leiningen, in Leiningen's word, and in Leiningen's wisdom, that they received his curt tidings, and his orders for the imminent struggle, with the calmness with which they were given. They waited, unafraid, alert, as if for the beginning of a new game or hunt which he had just described to them. The ants were indeed mighty, but not so mighty as the boss. Let them come!

They came at noon the second day. Their approach was announced by the wild unrest of the horses, scarcely controllable now either in stall or under rider, scenting from afar a vapor instinct with horror.

It was announced by a stampede of animals, timid and savage, hurtling past each other; jaguars and pumas flashing by nimble stags of the pampas, bulky tapirs, no longer hunters, themselves hunted, outpacing fleet kinkajous, maddened herds of cattle, heads lowered, nostrils snorting, rushing through tribes of loping monkeys, chattering in a dementia of terror; then followed the creeping and springing denizens of bush and steppe, big and little rodents, snakes, and lizards.

Pell-mell the rabble swarmed down the hill to the plantation, scattered right and left before the barrier of the water-filled ditch, then sped onwards to the river, where, again hindered, they fled along its bank out of sight.

This water-filled ditch was one of the defense measures

which Leiningen had long since prepared against the advent of the ants. It encompassed three sides of the plantation like a huge horseshoe. Twelve feet across, but not very deep, when dry it could hardly be described as an obstacle to either man or beast. But the ends of the "horseshoe" ran into the river which formed the northern boundary, and fourth side, of the plantation. And at the end nearer the house and outbuildings in the middle of the plantation, Leiningen had constructed a dam by means of which water from the river could be diverted into the ditch.

So now, by opening the dam, he was able to fling an imposing girdle of water, a huge quadrilateral with the river as its base, completely around the plantation, like the moat encircling a medieval city. Unless the ants were clever enough to build rafts, they had no hope of reaching the plantation, Leiningen concluded.

The twelve-foot water ditch seemed to afford in itself all the security needed. But while awaiting the arrival of the ants, Leiningen made a further improvement. The western section of the ditch ran along the edge of a tamarind wood, and the branches of some great trees reached over the water. Leiningen now had them lopped so that ants could not descend from them within the "moat."

The women and children, then the herds of cattle, were escorted by peons on rafts over the river, to remain on the other side in absolute safety until the plunderers had departed. Leiningen gave this instruction, not because he believed the non-combatants were in any danger, but in order to avoid hampering the efficiency of the defenders. "Critical situations first become crises," he explained to his men, "when oxen or women get excited."

Finally, he made a careful inspection of the "inner moat"—a smaller ditch lined with concrete, which extended around the hill on which stood the ranchhouse, barns, stables and other buildings. Into this concrete ditch emptied the inflow pipes from three great petrol tanks. If by some miracle the ants managed to cross the water and reach the plantation, this "rampart of petrol" would be an absolutely impassable protection for the besieged and their dwellings and stock. Such, at least, was Leiningen's opinion.

He stationed his men at irregular distances along the water ditch, the first line of defense. Then he lay down in his hammock and puffed drowsily away at his pipe until a peon came with the report that the ants had been observed far away in the South.

Leiningen mounted his horse, which at the feel of its master seemed to forget its uneasiness and rode leisurely in the direction of the threatening offensive. The southern stretch of ditch—the upper side of the quadrilateral—was nearly three miles long; from its center one could survey the entire countryside. This was destined to be the scene of the outbreak of war between Leiningen's brain and twenty square miles of life-destroying ants.

It was a sight one could never forget. Over the range of hills, as far as eye could see, crept a darkening hem, ever longer and broader, until the shadow spread across the slope from east to west, then downwards, downwards, uncannily swift, and all the green herbage of that wide vista was being mown as if by a giant sickle, leaving only the vast moving shadow, extending, deepening, and moving rapidly nearer.

When Leiningen's men, behind their barrier of water, perceived the approach of the long-expected foe, they gave vent to their suspense in screams and imprecations. But as the distance began to lessen between the "sons of hell" and the water ditch, they relapsed into silence. Before the advance of that awe-inspiring throng, their belief in the powers of the boss began to steadily dwindle. Even Leiningen himself, who had ridden up just in time to restore their loss of heart by a display of unshakable calm, even he could not free himself from a qualm of malaise. Yonder were thousands of millions of voracious jaws bearing down upon him and only a suddenly insignificant narrow ditch lay between him and his men and being gnawed to the bones "before you can spit three times."

Hadn't his brain for once taken on more than it could manage? If the blighters decided to rush the ditch, fill it to the brim with their corpses, there'd still be more than enough to destroy every trace of that cranium of his. The planter's chin jutted; they hadn't got him yet, and he'd see to it they never would. While he could think at all, he'd flout both death and the devil.

The hostile army was approaching in perfect formation; no human battalions, however well-drilled, could ever hope to rival the precision of that advance. Along a front that moved forward as uniformly as a straight line, the ants drew nearer and nearer to the water-ditch. Then, when they learned through their scouts the nature of the obstacle, the two outlying wings of the army detached themselves from the main body and marched down the western and eastern sides of the ditch.

This surrounding maneuver took rather more than an hour to accomplish; no doubt the ants expected that at some point they would find a crossing.

During this outflanking movement by the wings, the army on the center and southern front remained still. The besieged were therefore able to contemplate at their leisure the thumb-long, reddish black, long-legged insects; some of the Indians believed they could see, too, intent on them, the brilliant, cold eyes, and the razor-edged mandibles, of this host of infinity.

It is not easy for the average person to imagine that an animal, not to mention an insect, can *think*. But now both the European brain of Leiningen and the primitive brains of the Indians began to stir with the unpleasant foreboding that inside every single one of that deluge of insects dwelt a thought. And that thought was: Ditch or no ditch, we'll get to your flesh!

Not until four o'clock did the wings reach the "horseshoe" ends of the ditch, only to find these ran into the great river. Through some kind of secret telegraphy, the report must then have flashed very swiftly indeed along the entire enemy line. And Leiningen, riding—no longer casually—along his side of the ditch, noticed by energetic and widespread movements of troops that for some unknown reason the news of the check had its greatest effect on the southern front, where the main army was massed.

Perhaps the failure to find a way over the ditch was persuading the ants to withdraw from the plantation in search of spoils more easily obtainable.

An immense flood of ants, about a hundred yards in width, was pouring in a glimmering-black cataract down the far slope of the ditch. Many thousands were already drowning in the sluggish creeping flow, but they were followed by troop after troop, who clambered over their sinking comrades, and then themselves served as dying bridges to the reserves hurrying on in their rear.

Shoals of ants were being carried away by the current into the middle of the ditch, where gradually they broke asunder and then, exhausted by their struggles, vanished below the surface. Nevertheless, the wavering, floundering hundred-yard front was remorselessly if slowly advancing towards the besieged on the other bank. Leiningen had been wrong when he supposed the enemy would first have to fill the dtich with their bodies before they could cross; instead, they merely needed to act as stepping-stones, as they swam and sank, to the hordes ever pressing onwards from behind.

Near Leiningen a few mounted herdsmen awaited his orders. He sent one to the weir—the river must be dammed more strongly to increase the speed and power of the water coursing through the ditch.

A second peon was dispatched to the outhouses to bring spades and petrol sprinklers. A third rode away to summon to the zone of the offensive all the men, except the observation posts, on the near-by sections of the ditch, which were not yet actively threatened.

The ants were getting across far more quickly than Leiningen would have deemed possible. Impelled by the mighty cascade behind them, they struggled nearer and nearer to the inner bank. The momentum of the attack was so great that neither the tardy flow of the stream nor its downward pull could exert its proper force; and into the gap left by every submerging insect, hastened forward a dozen more.

When reinforcements reached Leiningen, the invaders were halfway over. The planter had to admit to himself

that it was only by a stroke of luck for him that the ants
were attempting the crossing on a relatively short front;
had they assaulted simultaneously along the entire length
of the ditch, the outlook for the defenders would have
been black indeed.

Even as it was, it could hardly be described as rosy,
though the planter seemed quite unaware that death in a
gruesome form was drawing closer and closer. As the war
between his brain and the "act of God" reached its cli-
max, the very shadow of annihilation began to pale to
Leiningen, who now felt like a champion in a new Olym-
pic game, a gigantic and thrilling contest, from which he
was determined to emerge victor. Such, indeed, was his
aura of confidence that the Indians forgot their stupefied
fear of the peril only a yard or two away; under the planter's supervision, they began fervidly digging up to the edge
of the bank and throwing clods of earth and spadefuls of sand into the midst of the hostile fleet.

The petrol sprinklers, hitherto used to destroy pests and
blights on the plantation, were also brought into action.
Streams of evil-reeking oil now soared and fell over an
enemy already in disorder through the bombardment of
earth and sand.

The ants responded to these vigorous and successful
measures of defense by further developments of their
offensive. Entire clumps of huddling insects began to roll
down the opposite bank into the water. At the same time,
Leiningen noticed that the ants were now attacking along
an ever-widening front. As the numbers both of his men
and his petrol sprinklers were severely limited, this rapid
extension of the line of battle was becoming an overwhelming danger.

To add to his difficulties, the very clods of earth they
flung into that black floating carpet often whirled fragments towards the defender's side, and here and there
dark ribbons were already mounting the inner bank.
True, wherever a man saw these they could still be driven
back into the water by spadefuls of earth or jets of petrol.
But the file of defenders was too sparse and scattered to
hold off at all points these landing parties, and though

the peons toiled like madmen, their plight became momently more perilous.

One man struck with his spade at an enemy clump, did not draw it back quickly enough from the water; in a trice the wooden haft swarmed with upward scurrying insects. With a curse, he dropped the spade into the ditch; too late, they were already on his body. They lost no time; wherever they encountered bare flesh they bit deeply; a few, bigger than the rest, carried in their hindquarters a sting which injected a burning and paralyzing venom. Screaming, frantic with pain, the peon danced and twirled like a dervish.

Realizing that another such casualty, yes, perhaps this alone, might plunge his men into confusion and destroy their morale, Leiningen roared in a bellow louder than the yells of the victim: "Into the petrol, idiot! Douse your paws in the petrol!" The dervish ceased his pirouette as if transfixed, then tore off his shirt and plunged his arm and the ants hanging to it up to the shoulder in one of the large open tins of petrol. But even then the fierce mandibles did not slacken; another peon had to help him squash and detach each separate insect.

Distracted by the episode, some defenders had turned away from the ditch. And now cries of fury, a thudding of spades, and a wild trampling to and fro, showed that the ants had made full use of the interval, though luckily only a few had managed to get across. The men set to work again desperately with the barrage of earth and sand. Meanwhile an old Indian, who acted as medicineman to the plantation workers, gave the bitten peon a drink he had prepared some hours before, which, he claimed, possessed the virtue of dissolving and weakening ants' venom.

Leiningen surveyed his position. A dispassionate observer would have estimated the odds against him at a thousand to one. But then such an onlooker would have reckoned only by what he saw—the advance of myriad battalions of ants against the futile efforts of a few defenders—and not by the unseen activity that can go on in a man's brain.

For Leiningen had not erred when he decided he would fight elemental with elemental. The water in the ditch was beginning to rise; the stronger damming of the river was making itself apparent.

Visibly the swiftness and power of the masses of water increased, swirling into quicker and quicker movement its living black surface, dispersing its pattern, carrying away more and more of it on the hastening current.

Victory had been snatched from the very jaws of defeat. With a hysterical shout of joy, the peons feverishly intensified their bombardment of earth clods and sand.

And now the wide cataract down the opposite bank was thinning and ceasing, as if the ants were becoming aware that they could not attain their aim. They were scurrying back up the slope to safety.

All the troops so far hurled into the ditch had been sacrificed in vain. Drowned and floundering insects eddied in thousands along the flow, while Indians running on the bank destroyed every swimmer that reached the side.

Not until the ditch curved towards the east did the scattered ranks assemble again in a coherent mass. And now, exhausted and half-numbed, they were in no condition to ascend the bank. Fusillades of clods drove them round the bend towards the mouth of the ditch and then into the river, wherein they vanished without leaving a trace.

The news ran swiftly along the entire chain of outposts, and soon a long scattered line of laughing men could be seen hastening along the ditch towards the scene of victory.

For once they seemed to have lost all their native reserve, for it was in wild abandon now they celebrated the triumph—as if there were no longer thousands of millions of merciless, cold and hungry eyes watching them from the opposite bank, watching and waiting.

The sun sank behind the rim of the tamarind wood and twilight deepened into night. It was not only hoped but expected that the ants would remain quiet until dawn. But to defeat any forlorn attempt at a crossing, the flow

of water through the ditch was powerfully increased by
opening the dam still further.

In spite of this impregnable barrier, Leiningen was not
yet altogether convinced that the ants would not venture
another surprise attack. He ordered his men to camp
along the bank overnight. He also detailed parties of
them to patrol the ditch in two of his motor cars and
ceaselessly to illuminate the surface of the water with
headlights and electric torches.

After having taken all the precautions he deemed necessary, the farmer ate his supper with considerable appe-
tite and went to bed. His slumbers were in no wise disturbed by the memory of the waiting, live, twenty square
miles.

Dawn found a thoroughly refreshed and active Leiningen riding along the edge of the ditch. The planter saw
before him a motionless and unaltered throng of besiegers. He studied the wide belt of water between them and
the plantation, and for a moment almost regretted that
the fight had ended so soon and so simply. In the com-
forting, matter-of-fact light of morning, it seemed to him
now that the ants hadn't the ghost of a chance to cross the
ditch. Even if they plunged headlong into it on all three
fronts at once, the force of the now powerful current
would inevitably sweep them away. He had got quite a
thrill out of the fight—a pity it was already over.

He rode along the eastern and southern sections of the
ditch and found everything in order. He reached the western section, opposite the tamarind wood, and here,
contrary to the other battle fronts, he found the enemy
very busy indeed. The trunks and branches of the trees
and the creepers of the lianas, on the far bank of the
ditch, fairly swarmed with industrious insects. But instead
of eating the leaves there and then, they were merely
gnawing through the stalks, so that a thick green shower
fell steadily to the ground.

No doubt they were victualing columns sent out to ob-
tain provender for the rest of the army. The discovery
did not surprise Leiningen. He did not need to be told
that ants are intelligent, that certain species even use oth-

ers as milch cows, watchdogs and slaves. He was well
aware of their power of adaptation, their sense of disci-
pline, their marvelous talent for organization.

His belief that a foray to supply the army was in progress was strengthened when he saw the leaves that fell to
the ground being dragged to the troops waiting outside
the wood. Then all at once he realized the aim that rain
of green was intended to serve.

Each single leaf, pulled or pushed by dozens of toiling
insects, was borne straight to the edge of the ditch. Even
as Macbeth watched the approach of Birnam Wood in
the hands of his enemies, Leiningen saw the tamarind
wood move nearer and nearer in the mandibles of the
ants. Unlike the fey Scot, however, he did not lose his
nerve; no witches had prophesied his doom, and if they
had he would have slept just as soundly. All the same, he
was forced to admit to himself that the situation was now
far more ominous than that of the day before.

He had thought it impossible for the ants to build rafts
for themselves—well, here they were, coming in thousands, more than enough to bridge the ditch. Leaves after
leaves rustled down the slope into the water, where the
current drew them away from the bank and carried them
into midstream. And every single leaf carried several
ants. This time the farmer did not trust to the alacrity of
his messengers. He galloped away, leaning from his sad-
dle and yelling orders as he rushed past outpost after outpost: "Bring petrol pumps to the southwest front! Issue
spades to every man along the line facing the wood!"
And arrived at the eastern and southern sections, he dispatched every man except the observation posts to the
menaced west.

Then, as he rode past the stretch where the ants had
failed to cross the day before, he witnessed a brief but
impressive scene. Down the slope of the distant hill there
came towards him a singular being, writhing rather than
running, an animal-like blackened statue with a shapeless
head and four quivering feet that knuckled under almost
ceaselessly. When the creature reached the far bank of

ditch and collapsed opposite Leiningen, he recognized it as a pampas stag, covered over and over with ants.

It had strayed near the zone of the army. As usual, they had attacked its eyes first. Blinded, it had reeled in the madness of hideous torment straight into the ranks of its persecutors, and now the beast swayed to and fro in its death agony.

With a shot from his rifle Leiningen put it out of its misery. Then he pulled out his watch. He hadn't a second to lose, but for life itself he could not have denied his curiosity the satisfaction of knowing how long the ants would take—for personal reasons, so to speak. After six minutes the white polished bones alone remained. That's how he himself would look before you can—. Leiningen spat once, and put spurs to his horse.

The sporting zest with which the excitement of the novel contest had inspired him the day before had now vanished; in its place was a cold and violent purpose. He would send these vermin back to the hell where they belonged, somehow, anyhow. Yes, but how was indeed the question; as things stood at present it looked as if the devils would raze him and his men from the earth instead. He had underestimated the might of the enemy; he really would have to bestir himself if he hoped to outwit them.

The biggest danger now, he decided, was the point where the western section of the ditch curved southwards. And arrived there, he found his worst expectations justified. The very power of the current had huddled the leaves and their crews of ants so close together at the bend that the bridge was almost ready.

True, streams of petrol and clumps of earth still prevented a landing. But the number of floating leaves was increasing ever more swiftly. It could not be long now before a stretch of water a mile in length was decked by a green pontoon over which the ants could rush in millions.

Leiningen galloped to the weir. The damming of the river was controlled by a wheel on its bank. The planter ordered the man at the wheel first to lower the water in the ditch almost to vanishing point, next to wait a moment, then suddenly to let the river in again. This maneuver of lowering and raising the surface, of decreasing then increasing the flow of water through the ditch was to be repeated over and over again until further notice.

This tactic was at first successful. The water in the ditch sank, and with it the film of leaves. The green fleet nearly reached the bed and the troops on the far bank swarmed down the slope to it. Then a violent flow of water at the original depth raced through the ditch, overwhelming leaves and ants, and sweeping them along.

This intermittent rapid flushing prevented just in time the almost completed fording of the ditch. But it also flung here and there squads of the enemy vanguard simultaneously up the inner bank. These seemed to know their duty only too well, and lost no time accomplishing it. The air rang with the curses of bitten Indians. They had removed their shirts and pants to detect the quicker the upwards-hastening insects; when they saw one, they crushed it; and fortunately the onslaught as yet was only by skirmishers.

Again and again, the water sank and rose, carrying leaves and drowned ants away with it. It lowered once more nearly to its bed; but this time the exhausted defenders waited in vain for the flush of destruction. Leiningen sensed disaster; something must have gone wrong with the machinery of the dam. Then a sweating peon tore up to him—

"They're over!"

While the besieged were concentrating upon the defense of the stretch opposite the wood, the seemingly unaffected line beyond the wood had become the theater of decisive action. Here the defenders' front was sparse and scattered; everyone who could be spared had hurried away to the south.

Just as the man at the weir had lowered the water almost to the bed of the ditch, the ants on a wide front began another attempt at a direct crossing like that of the preceding day. Into the emptied bed poured an irresistible throng. Rushing across the ditch, they attained the inner bank before the slow-witted Indians fully grasped the situation. Their frantic screams dumbfounded the man at the weir. Before he could direct the river anew into the safeguarding bed he saw himself surrounded by raging ants. He ran like the others, ran for his life.

When Leiningen heard this, he knew the plantation was doomed. He wasted no time bemoaning the inevitable. For as long as there was the slightest chance of success, he had stood his ground, and now any further resistance was both useless and dangerous. He fired three revolver shots into the air—the prearranged signal for his men to retreat instantly within the "inner moat." Then he rode towards the ranchhouse.

This was two miles from the point of invasion. There was therefore time enough to prepare the second line of defense against the advent of the ants. Of the three great petrol cisterns near the house, one had already been half emptied by the constant withdrawals needed for the pumps during the fight at the water ditch. The remaining petrol in it was now drawn off through underground pipes into the concrete trench which encircled the ranchhouse and its outbuildings.

And there, drifting in twos and threes, Leiningen's men reached him. Most of them were obviously trying to preserve an air of calm and indifference, belied, however, by their restless glances and knitted brows. One could see their belief in a favorable outcome of the struggle was already considerably shaken.

The planter called his peons around him.

"Well, lads," he began, "we've lost the first round. But we'll smash the beggars yet, don't you worry. Anyone who thinks otherwise can draw his pay here and now and push off. There are rafts enough and to spare on the river, and plenty of time still to reach 'em."

Not a man stirred.

Leiningen acknowledged his silent vote of confidence with a laugh that was half a grunt. "That's the stuff, lads. Too bad if you'd missed the rest of the show, eh? Well, the fun won't start till morning. Once these blighters turn tail, there'll be plenty of work for everyone and higher

wages all round. And now run along and get something
to eat; you've earned it all right."

In the excitement of the fight the greater part of the
day had passed without the men once pausing to snatch a
bite. Now that the ants were for the time being out of
sight, and the "wall of petrol" gave a stronger feeling of
security, hungry stomachs began to assert their claims.

The bridges over the concrete ditch were removed.
Here and there solitary ants had reached the ditch; they
gazed at the patrol meditatively, then scurried back again.
Apparently they had little interest at the moment for what
lay beyond the evil-reeking barrier; the abundant spoils of
the plantation were the main attraction. Soon the trees,
shrubs and beds for miles around were hulled with ants
zealously gobbling the yield of long weary months of
strenuous toil.

As twilight began to fall, a cordon of ants marched
around the petrol trench, but as yet made no move towards its brink. Leiningen posted sentries with headlights
and electric torches, then withdrew to his office, and
began to reckon up his losses. He estimated these as
large, but, in comparison with his bank balance, by no
means unbearable. He worked out in some detail a
scheme of intense cultivation which would enable him,
before very long, to more than compensate himself for
the damage now being wrought to his crops. It was with a
contented mind that he finally betook himself to bed
where he slept deeply until dawn, undisturbed by any
thought that next day little more might be left to him
than a glistening skeleton.

He rose with the sun and went out on the flat roof of
his house. And a scene like one from Dante lay around
him; for miles in every direction there was nothing but a
black, glittering multitude, a multitude of rested, sated,
but none the less voracious ants: yes, look as far as one
might, one could see nothing but that rustling black
throng, except in the north, where the great river drew a
boundary they could not hope to pass. But even the high
stone breakwater, along the bank of the river, which Leiningen had built as a defense against inundations, was,

like the paths, the shorn trees and shrubs, the ground itself, black with ants.

So their greed was not glutted in razing that vast plantation? Not by a long chalk; they were all the more eager now on a rich and certain booty—four hundred men, numerous horses, and bursting granaries.

At first it seemed that the petrol trench would serve its purpose. The besiegers sensed the peril of swimming it, and made no move to plunge blindly over its brink. Instead they devised a better maneuver; they began to collect shreds of bark, twigs and dried leaves and dropped these into the petrol. Everything green, which could have been similarly used, had long since been eaten. After a time, though, a long procession could be seen bringing from the west the tamarind leaves used as rafts the day before.

Since the petrol, unlike the water in the outer ditch, was perfectly still, the refuse stayed where it was thrown. It was several hours before the ants succeeded in covering an appreciable part of the surface. At length, however, they were ready to proceed to a direct attack.

Their storm troops swarmed down the concrete side, scrambled over the supporting surface of twigs and leaves, and impelled these over the few remaining streaks of open petrol until they reached the other side. Then they began to climb up this to make straight for the helpless garrison.

During the entire offensive, the planter sat peacefully, watching them with interest, but not stirring a muscle. Moreover, he had ordered his men not to disturb in any way whatever the advancing horde. So they squatted listlessly along the bank of the ditch and waited for a sign from the boss.

The petrol was now covered with ants. A few had climbed the inner concrete wall and were scurrying towards the defenders.

"Everyone back from the ditch!" roared Leiningen. The men rushed away, without the slightest idea of his plan. He stooped forward and cautiously dropped into the ditch a stone which split the floating carpet and its living freight, to reveal a gleaming patch of petrol. A match spurted, sank down to the oily surface—Leiningen sprang back; in a flash a towering rampart of fire encompassed the garrison.

This spectacular and instant repulse threw the Indians into ecstasy. They applauded, yelled and stamped, like children at a pantomime. Had it not been for the awe in which they held the boss, they would infallibly have carried him shoulder high.

It was some time before the petrol burned down to the bed of the ditch, and the wall of smoke and flame began to lower. The ants had retreated in a wide circle from the devastation, and innumerable charred fragments along the outer bank showed that the flames had spread from the holocaust in the ditch well into the ranks beyond, where they had wrought havoc far and wide.

Yet the perseverance of the ants was by no means broken; indeed, each setback seemed only to whet it. The concrete cooled, the flicker of the dying flames wavered and vanished, petrol from the second tank poured into the trench—and the ants marched forward anew to the attack.

The foregoing scene repeated itself in every detail, except that on this occasion less time was needed to bridge the ditch, for the petrol was now already filmed by a layer of ash. Once again they withdrew; once again petrol flowed into the ditch. Would the creatures never learn that their self-sacrifice was utterly senseless? It really was senseless, wasn't it? Yes, of course it was senseless—provided the defenders had an *unlimited* supply of petrol.

When Leiningen reached this stage of reasoning, he felt for the first time since the arrival of the ants that his confidence was deserting him. His skin began to creep; he loosened his collar. Once the devils were over the trench there wasn't a chance in hell for him and his men. God, what a prospect, to be eaten alive like that!

For the third time the flames immolated the attacking troops, and burned down to extinction. Yet the ants were coming on again as if nothing had happened. And meanwhile Leiningen had made a discovery that chilled him to the bone—petrol was no longer flowing into the ditch. Something must be blocking the outflow pipe of the third and last cistern—a snake or a dead rat? Whatever it was, the ants could be held off no longer, unless petrol could by some method be led from the cistern into the ditch.

Then Leiningen remembered that in an outhouse nearby were two old disused fire engines. Spry as never before in their lives, the peons dragged them out of the shed, connected their pumps to the cistern, uncoiled and laid the hose. They were just in time to aim a stream of petrol at a column of ants that had already crossed and drive them back down the incline into the ditch. Once more an oily girdle surrounded the garrison, once more it was possible to hold the position—for the moment.

It was obvious, however, that this last resource meant only the postponement of defeat and death. A few of the peons fell on their knees and began to pray; others shrieking insanely, fired their revolvers at the black, advancing masses, as if they felt their despair was pitiful enough to sway fate itself to mercy.

At length, two of the men's nerves broke: Leiningen saw a naked Indian leap over the north side of the petrol trench, quickly followed by a second. They sprinted with incredible speed towards the river. But their fleetness did not save them; long before they could attain the rafts, the enemy covered their bodies from head to foot.

In the agony of their torment, both sprang blindly into the wide river, where enemies no less sinister awaited them. Wild screams of mortal anguish informed the breathless onlookers that crocodiles and sword-tooth piranhas were no less ravenous than ants, and even nimbler in reaching their prey.

In spite of this bloody warning, more and more men showed they were making up their minds to run the blockade. Anything, even a fight midstream against alligators, seemed better than powerlessly waiting for death to come and slowly consume their living bodies.

Leiningen flogged his brain till it reeled. Was there nothing on earth could sweep this devils' spawn back into the hell from which it came?

Then out of the inferno of his bewilderment rose a ter-rifying inspiration. Yes, one hope remained, and one alone. It might be possible to dam the great river completely, so that its waters would fill not only the water ditch but overflow into the entire gigantic "saucer" of land in which lay the plantation.

The far bank of the river was too high for the waters to escape that way. The stone breakwater ran between the river and the plantation; its only gaps occurred where the "horseshoe" ends of the water-ditch passed into the river. So its waters would not only be forced to inundate into the plantation, they would also be held there by the breakwater until they rose to its own high level. In half an hour, perhaps even earlier, the plantation and its hos-tile army of occupation would be flooded.

The ranch house and outbuildings stood upon rising ground. Their foundations were higher than the breakwa-ter, so the flood would not reach them. And any remaining ants trying to ascend the slope could be repulsed by pe-trol.

It was possible—yes, if one could only get to the dam! A distance of nearly two miles lay between the ranch house and the weir—two miles of ants. Those two peons had managed only a fifth of that distance at the cost of their lives. Was there an Indian daring enough after that to run the gauntlet five times as far? Hardly likely; and if there were, his prospect of getting back was almost nil.

No, there was only one thing for it, he'd have to make the attempt himself; he might just as well be running as sitting still, anyway, when the ants finally got him. Be-sides, there was a bit of a chance. Perhaps the ants weren't so almighty, after all; perhaps he had allowed the mass suggestion of that evil black throng to hypnotize him, just as a snake fascinates and overpowers.

The ants were building their bridges. Leiningen got up on a chair. "Hey, lads, listen to me," he cried. Slowly and listlessly, from all sides of the trench, the men began to shuffle towards him, the apathy of death already stamped on their faces.

"Listen, lads!" he shouted. "You're frightened of those

beggars, but you're a damn sight more frightened of me, and I'm proud of you. There's still a chance to save our lives—by flooding the plantation from the river. Now one of you might manage to get as far as the weir—but he'd never come back. Well, I'm not going to let you try it; if I did I'd be worse than one of those ants. No. I called the tune, and now I'm going to pay the piper.

"The moment I'm over the ditch, set fire to the petrol. That'll allow time for the flood to do the trick. Then all you have to do is to wait here all snug and quiet till I'm back. Yes, I'm coming back, trust me"—he grinned—"when I've finished my slimming-cure."

He pulled on high leather boots, drew heavy gauntlets over his hands, and stuffed the spaces between breeches and boots, gauntlets and arms, shirt and neck, with rags soaked in petrol. With close-fitting mosquito goggles he shielded his eyes, knowing too well the ants' dodge of first robbing their victim of sight. Finally, he plugged his nostrils and ears with cottonwool, and let the peons drench his clothes with petrol.

He was about to set off, when the old Indian medicine man came up to him; he had a wondrous salve, he said, prepared from a species of chafer whose odor was intolerable to ants. Yes, this odor protected these chafers from the attacks of even the most murderous ants. The Indian smeared the boss' boots, his gauntlets, and his face over and over with the extract.

Leiningen then remembered the paralyzing effect of ants' venom, and the Indian gave him a gourd full of the medicine he had administered to the bitten peon at the water ditch. The planter drank it down without noticing its bitter taste; his mind was already at the weir.

He started off towards the northwest corner of the trench. With a bound he was over—and among the ants.

The beleaguered garrison had no opportunity to watch Leiningen's race against death. The ants were climbing the inner bank again—the lurid ring of petrol blazed aloft. For the fourth time that day the reflection from the fire shone on the sweating faces of the imprisoned men, and on the reddish-black cuirasses of their oppressors.

The red and blue, dark-edged flames leaped vividly now, celebrating what? The funeral pyre of the four hundred, or of the hosts of destruction?

Leiningen ran. He ran in long equal strides, with only one thought, one sensation, in his being—he *must* get through. He dodged all trees and shrubs; except for the split seconds his soles touched the ground the ants should have no opportunity to alight on him. That they would get to him soon, despite the salve on his boots, the petrol in his clothes, he realized only too well, but he knew even more surely that he must, and that he would, get to the weir.

Apparently the salve was some use after all; not until he had reached halfway did he feel ants under his clothes, and a few on his face. Mechanically, in his stride, he struck at them, scarcely conscious of their bites. He saw he was drawing appreciably near the weir—the distance grew less and less—sank to five hundred—three—two—one hundred yards.

Then he was at the weir and gripping the ant-hulled wheel. Hardly had he seized it when a horde of infuriated ants flowed over his hands, arms and shoulders. He started the wheel—before it turned once on its axis the swarm covered his face. Leiningen strained like a madman, his lips pressed tight; if he opened them to draw breath . . .

He turned and turned; slowly the dam lowered until it reached the bed of the river. Already the water was overflowing the ditch. Another minute, and the river was pouring through the near-by gap in the breakwater. The flooding of the plantation had begun.

Leiningen let go the wheel. Now, for the first time, he realized he was coated from head to foot with a layer of ants. In spite of the petrol, his clothes were full of them, several had got to his body and were clinging to his face. Now that he had completed his task, he felt the smart raging over his flesh from the bites of sawing and piercing insects.

Frantic with pain, he almost plunged into the river. To be ripped and slashed to shreds by piranhas? Already he was running the return journey, knocking ants from his gloves and jacket, brushing them from his bloodied face, squashing them to death under his clothes.

One of the creatures bit him just below the rim of his goggles; he managed to tear it away, but the agony of the bite and its etching acid drilled into the eye nerves; he saw now through circles of fire into a milky mist, then he ran for a time almost blinded, knowing that if he once tripped and fell . . . The old Indian's brew didn't seem much good; it weakened the poison a bit, but didn't get rid of it. His heart pounded as if it would burst; blood roared in his ears; a giant's fist battered his lungs.

Then he could see again, but the burning girdle of petrol appeared infinitely far away; he could not last half that distance. Swift-changing pictures flashed through his head, episodes in his life, while in another part of his brain a cool and impartial onlooker informed this ant-blurred, gasping, exhausted bundle named Leiningen that such a rushing panorama of scenes from one's past is seen only in the moment before death.

A stone in the path . . . too weak to avoid it . . . the planter stumbled and collapsed. He tried to rise . . . he must be pinned under a rock . . . It was impossible . . . the slightest movement was impossible . . .

Then all at once he saw, starkly clear and huge, and, right before his eyes, furred with ants, towering and swaying in its death agony, the pampas stag. In six minutes—gnawed to the bones. God, he *couldn't* die like that! And something outside him seemed to drag him to his feet. He tottered. He began to stagger forward again.

Through the blazing ring hurtled an apparition which, as soon as it reached the ground on the inner side, fell full length and did not move. Leiningen, at the moment he made that leap through the flames, lost consciousness for the first time in his life. As he lay there, with glazing eyes and lacerated face, he appeared a man returned from the grave. The peons rushed to him, stripped off his clothes, tore away the ants from a body that seemed almost one open wound; in some places the bones were showing. They carried him into the ranch house.

As the curtain of flames lowered, one could see in place

of the illimitable host of ants an extensive vista of water. The thwarted river had swept over the plantation, carrying with it the entire army. The water had collected and mounted in a great "saucer," while the ants had in vain attempted to reach the hill on which stood the ranch house. The girdle of flames held them back.

And so imprisoned between water and fire, they had been delivered into the annihilation that was their god. And near the farther mouth of the water-ditch, where the stone mole had its second gap, the ocean swept the lost battalions into the river, to vanish forever.

The ring of fire dwindled as the water mounted to the petrol trench, and quenched the dimming flames. The inundation rose higher and higher; because its outflow was impeded by the timber and underbrush it had carried along with it, its surface required some time to reach the top of the high stone breakwater and discharge over it the rest of the shattered army.

It swelled over ant-stippled shrubs and bushes, until it washed against the foot of the knoll whereon the besieged had taken refuge. For a while an alluvial of ants tried again and again to attain this dry land, only to be repulsed by streams of petrol back into the merciless flood.

Leiningen lay on his bed, his body swathed from head to foot in bandages. With fomentations and salves, they had managed to stop the bleeding, and had dressed his many wounds. Now they thronged around him, one question in every face. Would he recover? "He won't die," said the old man who had bandaged him, "if he doesn't want to."

The planter opened his eyes. "Everything in order?" he asked.

"They're gone," said his nurse. "To hell." He held out to his master a gourd full of a powerful sleeping draught. Leiningen gulped it down.

"I told you I'd come back," he murmured, "even if I am a bit streamlined." He grinned and shut his eyes. He slept.

JOURNALISM IN TENNESSEE

by Mark Twain

The editor of the Memphis *Avalanche* swoops thus mildly down upon a correspondent who posted him as a Radical:— "While he was writing the first word, the middle, dotting his i's, crossing his t's, and punching his period, he knew he was concocting a sentence that was saturated with infamy and reeking with falsehood."–*Exchange*.

I WAS TOLD BY THE PHYSICIAN that a Southern climate would improve my health, and so I went down to Tennessee, and got a berth on the *Morning Glory and Johnson County War-Whoop* as associate editor. When I went on duty I found the chief editor sitting tilted back in a three-legged chair with his feet on a pine table. There was another pine table in the room and another afflicted chair, and both were half buried under newspapers and scraps and sheets of manuscript. There was a wooden box of sand, sprinkled with cigar stubs and "old soldiers," and a stove with a door hanging by its upper hinge. The chief editor had a long-tailed black frock-coat on, and white linen pants. His boots were small and neatly blacked. He wore a ruffled shirt, a large seal-ring, a standing collar of obsolete pattern, and a checkered neckerchief with the ends hanging down. Date of costume about 1848. He was smoking a cigar, and trying to think of a word, and in pawing his hair he had rumpled his locks a good deal. He was scowling fearfully, and I judged that he was concocting a particularly knotty editorial. He told me to take the exchanges and skim through them and write up the "Spirit of the

Tennessee Press," condensing into the article all of their contents that seemed of interest.

I wrote as follows:

SPIRIT OF THE TENNESSEE PRESS

The editors of the *Semi-Weekly Earthquake* evidently labor under a misapprehension with regard to the Ballyhack railroad. It is not the object of the company to leave Buzzardville off to one side. On the contrary, they consider it one of the most important points along the line, and consequently can have no desire to slight it. The gentlemen of the *Earthquake* will, of course, take pleasure in making the correction.

John W. Blossom, Esq., the able editor of the Higginsville *Thunderbolt and Battle Cry of Freedom,* arrived in the city yesterday. He is stopping at the Van Buren House.

We observe that our contemporary of the Mud Springs *Morning Howl* has fallen into the error of supposing that the election of Van Werter is not an established fact, but he will have discovered his mistake before this reminder reaches him, no doubt. He was doubtless misled by incomplete election returns.

It is pleasant to note that the city of Blathersville is endeavoring to contract with some New York gentlemen to pave its well-nigh impassable streets with the Nicholson pavement. The *Daily Hurrah* urges the measure with ability, and seems confident of ultimate success.

I passed my manuscript over to the chief editor for acceptance, alteration, or destruction. He glanced at it and his face clouded. He ran his eye down the pages, and his countenance grew portentous. It was easy to see that something was wrong. Presently he sprang up and said:

"Thunder and lightning! Do you suppose I am going to speak of those cattle that way? Do you suppose my subscribers are going to stand such gruel as that? Give me the pen!"

I never saw a pen scrape and scratch its way so viciously, or plow through another man's verbs and adjectives so relentlessly. While he was in the midst of his work, somebody shot at him through the open window, and marred the symmetry of my ear.

"Ah," said he, "that is that scoundrel Smith, of the

Moral Volcano—he was due yesterday." And he snatched a navy revolver from his belt and fired. Smith dropped, shot in the thigh. The shot spoiled Smith's aim, who was just taking a second chance, and he crippled a stranger. It was me. Merely a finger shot off.

Then the chief editor went on with his erasures and interlineations. Just as he finished them a hand-grenade came down the stovepipe, and the explosion shivered the stove into a thousand fragments. However, it did no further damage, except that a vagrant piece knocked a couple of my teeth out.

"That stove is utterly ruined," said the chief editor.

I said I believed it was.

"Well, no matter—don't want it this kind of weather. I know the man that did it. I'll get him. Now, *here* is the way this stuff ought to be written."

I took the manuscript. It was scarred with erasures and interlineations till its mother wouldn't have known it if it had one. It now read as follows:

SPIRIT OF THE TENNESSEE PRESS

The inveterate liars of the *Semi-Weekly Earthquake* are evidently endeavoring to palm off upon a noble and chivalrous people another of their vile and brutal falsehoods with regard to that most glorious conception of the nineteenth century, the Ballyhack railroad. The idea that Buzzardville was to be left off at one side originated in their own fulsome brains—or rather in the settlings which *they* regard as brains. They had better swallow this lie if they want to save their abandoned reptile carcasses the cowhiding they so richly deserve.

That ass, Blossom, of the Higginsville *Thunderbolt and Battle Cry of Freedom,* is down here again sponging at the Van Buren.

We observe that the besotted blackguard of the Mud Springs *Morning Howl* is giving out, with his usual propensity for lying, that Van Werter is not elected. The heaven-born mission of journalism is to disseminate truth; to eradicate error; to educate, refine, and elevate the tone of public morals and manners, and make all men more gentle, more virtuous, more charitable, and in all ways better, and holier, and happier; and yet this black-hearted scoundrel degrades his great office persistently to the dissemination of falsehood, calumny, vituperation, and vulgarity.

Blathersville wants a Nicholson pavement—it wants a jail and a poorhouse more. The idea of a pavement in a one-horse town composed of two gin-mills, a blacksmith shop, and that mustard-plaster of a newspaper, the *Daily Hurrah!* The crawling insect, Buckner, who edits the *Hurrah,* is braying about his business with his customary imbecility, and imagining that he is talking sense.

"Now *that* is the way to write—peppery and to the point. Mush-and-milk journalism gives me the fan-tods."

About this time a brick came through the window with a splintering crash, and gave me a considerable jolt in the back. I moved out of range—I began to feel in the way.

The chief said, "That was the Colonel, likely. I've been expecting him for two days. He will be up now right away."

He was correct. The Colonel appeared in the door a moment afterward with a dragoon revolver in his hand.

He said, "Sir, have I the honor of addressing the poltroon who edits this mangy sheet?"

"You have. Be seated, sir. Be careful of the chair, one of its legs is gone. I believe I have the honor of addressing the putrid liar, Colonel Blatherskite Tecumseh?"

"Right, sir. I have a little account to settle with you. If you are at leisure we will begin."

"I have an article on the 'Encouraging Progress of Moral and Intellectual Development in America' to finish, but there is no hurry. Begin."

Both pistols rang out their fierce clamor at the same instant. The chief lost a lock of his hair, and the Colonel's bullet ended its career in the fleshy part of my thigh. The Colonel's left shoulder was clipped a little. They fired again. Both missed their men this time, but I got my share, a shot in the arm. At the third fire both gentlemen were wounded slightly, and I had a knuckle chipped. I then said, I believe I would go out and take a walk, as this was a private matter, and I had a delicacy about participating in it further. But both gentlemen begged me to keep my seat, and assured me that I was not in the way.

They then talked about the elections and the crops

while they reloaded, and I fell to tying up my wounds. But presently they opened fire again with animation, and every shot took effect—but it is proper to remark that five out of the six fell to my share. The sixth one mortally wounded the Colonel, who remarked, with fine humor, that he would have to say good morning now, as he had business uptown. He then inquired the way to the undertaker's and left.

The chief turned to me and said, "I am expecting company to dinner, and shall have to get ready. It will be a favor to me if you will read proof and attend to the customers."

I winced a little at the idea of attending to the customers, but I was too bewildered by the fusillade that was still ringing in my ears to think of anything to say.

He continued, "Jones will be here at three—cowhide him. Gillespie will call earlier, perhaps—throw him out of the window. Ferguson will be along about four—kill him. That is all for to-day, I believe. If you have any odd time, you may write a blistering article on the police—give the chief inspector rats. The cowhides are under the table; weapons in the drawer—ammunition there in the corner —lint and bandages up there in the pigeonholes. In case of accident, go to Lancet, the surgeon, down-stairs. He advertises—we take it out in trade."

He was gone. I shuddered. At the end of the next three hours I had been through perils so awful that all peace of mind and all cheerfulness were gone from me. Gillespie had called and thrown *me* out of the window. Jones arrived promptly, and when I got ready to do the cowhiding he took the job off my hands. In an encounter with a stranger, not in the bill of fare, I had lost my scalp. Another stranger, by the name of Thompson, left me a mere wreck and ruin of chaotic rags. And at last, at bay in the corner, and beset by an infuriated mob of editors, blacklegs, politicians, and desperadoes, who raved and swore and flourished their weapons about my head till the air shimmered with glancing flashes of steel, I was in the act of resigning my berth on the paper when the chief arrived, and with him a rabble of charmed and enthusiastic friends. Then ensued a scene of riot and carnage such as no human pen, or steel one either, could describe. People were shot, probed, dismembered, blown up, thrown out of the window. There was a brief tornado of murky blasphemy, with a confused and frantic war-dance glimmering through it, and then all was over. In five minutes there was silence, and the gory chief and I sat alone and surveyed the sanguinary ruin that strewed the floor around us.

He said, "You'll like this place when you get used to it."

I said, "I'll have to get you to excuse me; I think maybe I might write to suit you after a while; as soon as I have had some practice and learned the language I am confident I could. But, to speak the plain truth, that sort of energy of expression has its inconveniences, and a man is liable to interruption. You see that yourself. Vigorous writing is calculated to elevate the public, no doubt, but then I do not like to attract so much attention as it calls forth. I can't write with comfort when I am interrupted so much as I have been to-day. I like this berth well enough, but I don't like to be left here to wait on the customers. The experiences are novel, I grant you, and entertaining, too, after a fashion, but they are not judiciously distributed. A gentleman shoots at you through the window and cripples *me*; a bombshell comes down the stove-pipe for your gratification and sends the stove door down *my* throat; a friend drops in to swap compliments with you, and freckles *me* with bullet-holes till my skin won't hold my principles; you go to dinner, and Jones comes with his cowhide, Gillespie throws me out of the window, Thompson tears all my clothes off, and an entire stranger takes my scalp with the easy freedom of an old acquaintance; and in less than five minutes all the blackguards in the country arrive in their war-paint, and proceed to scare the rest of me to death with their tomahawks. Take it altogether, I never had such a spirited time in all my life as I have had to-day. No; I like you, and I like your calm unruffled way of explaining things to the customers, but you see I am not used to it. The Southern heart is too impulsive; Southern hospitality is too lavish with the stranger. The paragraphs which I have written to-day, and into whose cold sentences your masterly hand has infused the fervent spirit of Tennessean journalism, will wake up another nest of hornets. All that mob of editors will come—and they will come hungry, too, and want somebody for breakfast. I shall have to bid you adieu. I decline to be present at these festivities. I came South for my health, I will go back on the same errand, and suddenly. Tennessean journalism is too stirring for me."

After which we parted with mutual regret, and I took apartments at the hospital.

ALONE IN SHARK WATERS

by John Kruse

DOWN IN THE HOLD, the noise was earsplitting. Every timber, the length and breadth of the *Ben Sidi Tajir*, seemed to be shrieking in agony. The single hurricane lamp swung sickeningly overhead, swilling its anemic light around in the blackness. Mike Gardener shut his eyes and braced himself against a crate; he felt the ship lift and drop away crabwise in a quick, double movement that sucked his stomach about inside him like water in a goatskin.

The native passengers around him were now fully awake. They were sitting up among the cargo, chattering shrilly, the whites of their eyes showing clearly in the lamplight. There were about twenty of them, traveling freight, like himself, from Ceylon to the Maldive Islands

The *Ben Sidi Tajir* was a Maldivian schooner, and her run was between Colombo and the islands. She was a cross between a felucca and a Spanish galleon, and her crew was a ragged bunch of moplas, descended from the old Malabar Coast pirates. There was nothing those moplas didn't know about the sea. They had smelled the wind coming five hours before it hit the ship. The ship was a full day out of port. There was nothing they could do but keep running and hope to miss it. When the wind was an hour away, they knew by the sky that they didn't have a chance. It was two in the morning, and Mike was asleep on deck. They had shaken him awake and told him to get below. Then they had dropped the big triangular sail, battened down the hatches and heaved to.

The only passenger accommodation was the hold, and Mike had gone down there wondering what the panic was. He didn't wonder for long. It was a hurricane.

It hit the mainmast with a shock that went right down into the ship and set up a howl in the rigging that made Mike's hackles creep. The ship was half empty, and with all her galleonlike superstructure in the stern, she began to roll like a tar barrel.

Mike braced himself with his feet and listened to the grinding timbers and cursed. There were safer ways of getting to the islands than in this relic, but not as cheap; that was the rub. When you speared fish for a living, you couldn't afford to ride fancy.

He was on his way to the Maldives to try the spearing there. He was planning to fish his way through the reefs, selling his catches as he went—a sort of working vacation. His spear gun lay on the rice sacks beside him, with his fins and mask strapped to the trigger guard. His only other baggage was a pack containing a change of clothing, a dozen harpoon heads and a sixty-foot reel he used for spearing in deep water.

The storm seemed to be getting worse. He could hear the Diesel auxiliary laboring hard in the struggle to keep the ship's head into the wind, felt the screw race in the air each time she toppled down into a trough. Near him a mopla woman lay on the sacks clutching her belly and whimpering. She was pregnant, and Mike couldn't tell if she was in labor or just seasick. She didn't seem to belong to anybody. He spoke to her in Singhalese, but she made no sign that she had heard him.

Suddenly the ship gave one of its quick, double movements. There was a slow, grinding crash, and the vessel seemed to convulse. The lantern leaped from its hook, smashed against a crate and went out. Through the infernal din Mike heard the natives screaming and, in the blackness, felt the ship heave over on its side.

His instantaneous throught was that they had hit a reef. Then he knew they couldn't have. They were a full day's sail west of Ceylon; the water here was five hundred

fathoms deep. The ship was breaking up. He grabbed up
his most valuable possession, the spear gun, and struggled
toward the mopla woman. He fell across her and she
screamed. He shouted at her that it was the American
and, gripping her under the armpits, lifted her to her feet
and half carried, half dragged her toward where he knew
the gangway out of the hold to be.

The natives blundered together in the darkness,
screaming and groping for the doorway. A match spurted
near him. There was an instant of wild eyes and gleaming
bodies. He spotted the gangway. The match went out as
the crowd surged forward. The next moment, he and the
woman were caught up in a crazy, struggling mass. Someone grabbed onto his back, clawed a way up over him.
He kept hold of the woman and his gun, and shoved.

Suddenly something gave, and they were moving forward through water already knee deep. It was deluging
down from above, and there were figures up there against
a faint square of sky, trying to fight their way up through
the water, but it was forcing them back. Then the boat
rolled and the deluge stopped. Mike got the woman's
hand and clamped it onto his belt, then heaved himself up
onto the companionway. Someone got hold of his gun
and tried to pull him down by it. The gun was so long
that it was fouling everything, and he nearly decided to
let it go. Then he changed his mind. It was his livelihood,
and he had brought it all the way from Genoa.

He wrenched the gun free and struggled up the ladder.
There was someone above him; he lifted him by force
clean out on deck, fell on top of him, rolled over, and
reached back down the hatch for the woman. He got hold
of her by the hair just as a wave smashed down onto
them. It flattened him against the deck; if he hadn't had
hold of the woman, it would have knocked her off the
ladder. Someone screamed. The water dragged at him
and drained away. Mike gasped and opened his eyes.

The deck slanted right down into the sea; there were
no lights anywhere. The native beside him had disappeared. He had an impression of black mountains heaving against a sulphurous sky, of smashed rigging. Another

wave crashed down on him like a ton weight, but he had the woman under the arms now and her weight anchored him.

As the wave hissed away, Mike pulled her out and got her down beside him on the slanting deck. More natives stumbled up out of the hatch. He was trying to remember where the lifeboats were. But the onslaught had been so quick, the crew wouldn't have had a chance to launch them. Something was sticking into his belly. It was the gun, with the fins and mask attached to it. He picked it up and looked around for something that would float. There was a life belt against the deckhouse; he caught the gleam of it in the darkness.

He took the woman's arms and hooked them over the hatch. He waited for the ship to roll back and tried to run along the sloping deck. His plimsolls slipped. He hit the planking with a smack and began to slide.

Mike's mind cleared; beyond fear, coolly and carefully, he watched for the rail, preparing to check against it with his feet. Its silhouette stood out clearly a foot or two above the foam. Then something crashed down on top of him, and he was under water again, tons of it, black and heavy and solid. It burned up into his sinuses, filling his brain with stars. Then the weight seemed to lift, and he lifted with it, up and up and up. Then surprisingly, there was air. He gulped at it, opened his eyes, and saw the dark shape of the ship. It was below him. Scared that he would be smashed against it, he began to swim.

He swam with the wind, angling past the wreck. He was lifted and flung like a cork toward the tilted deck. A native was clinging to the rail. Mike was dashed to within a foot of him, and sucked back. He saw the shine of water on the man's back, saw him hanging in the sudden vacuum; then the sea heaved up and tore the native loose. He couldn't see what happened to him. The next moment, Mike was clear of the stern, surrounded by blackness, unable to see or to gauge the waves, trying to time his breaths to coincide with his rises to the surface. There was so much water in the air; it was difficult to tell when he was under and when he wasn't.

Hopelessness welled up in him. He was being swept away from the wreck into the raging blackness of the Indian Ocean. The nearest land was Ceylon, maybe a hundred miles to the east. He knew that no boat had got clear of the ship and that his chances of being picked up were nil. But he made no attempt to fight his way back to the vessel. If he had he would have been drowned inside of a minute, and instinctively he knew it. He kept right on with the storm, out into the vastness and the darkness. And he was afraid.

He struggled in the whirl and plunge of the waters, sobbing for air, trying to think. But he couldn't think of anything. He felt that something was dragging him under and realized that it was the spear gun. The mask and fins strapped to it were cupping the water. It was natural for him to have a gun; he didn't wonder about it any more than a carpenter would wonder about having his hammer. Its five pounds of duralumin and steel were a part of him; now they were gripped in his right hand in a clutch that nothing short of death could have broken.

The familiarity of the gun steadied him. It never occurred to him to drop it. He hugged it into his chest and kept swimming, and a process began in the back of his mind that suddenly became defiance. He was in the sea and he had the gun. It was the same sea—the sea that was his life, the sea that he dived and hunted in every day all day—whipped up now into a frenzy, but still the same sea. There were jokes in Colombo about his being half fish. Maybe he was. Well, this was his sea.

The idea grew, and the storm seemed to change; maybe it was really letting up—he didn't know, but he knew suddenly that he could beat it, the way a fighter can sometimes tell with his opponent the first moment he comes in against him. He could ride it out, and there would be a plane. They would be bound to send out a plane.

A big wave curled over on top of him from behind and buried him in darkness. He didn't fight it; he just lay in the water holding his breath. He felt himself falling. He was out of the back of it. He breathed until he felt the lift of the next one, gasped a lungful of air, and, as it broke over him, ripped off his pants and shoes. In the next wave he got rid of his shirt. He was naked now except for his belt and knife. He thought of trying to put his fins on, but he knew he could never make it.

He needed all the buoyancy he could get. With every gasp of air, he began to swallow some. He felt the bubbles form in his stomach and fought back the desire to belch them out again.

He wrestled the spear gun around to the small of his back and clipped the butt hook onto his belt, so that he had the use of both arms.

He could lie along the surface then. It was like body-surfing, only the waves weren't breaking, they were running. Instead of carrying him with them, they swept by underneath, lifting and dropping him, with a feet-to-head movement, so far and so fast he was jarred nearly senseless. The speed of the sea against the fins and mask drove the harpoon down between his legs and turned him over. He went under and nearly didn't come up.

He didn't want to jettison the gun, so he pulled around into the wind and faced the sea. The spray was wicked, but the movement was better. The gun behind him acted as a rudder.

Mike stayed that way, with the sea tearing past him, breaking through the waves, his mind stopped down to a pinpoint of concentration. Keep alive, he thought. Never mind where the wind is taking you. Just keep alive. Planes will scour the whole area. Ride it. Just ride it out. You've been in a spot before. How about Iwo Jima? What did you do then? Ride it out!

Wave after wave came—rush, rush, rush. The sounds dabbed and cleared in his ears monotonously, and it was the roaring and fading of sea shells, and then it was voices—loud, then soft. Then it was anesthesia, with great whirling lights and the punch-punch of watery fists in his eyes growing duller and, as time dragged by, imperceptible; he could feel nothing, and yet he knew it was still going on. There was movement and a sense of flying and sinking, but no feeling at all, nothing, and he got scared. He thought he was unconscious, that he was drowning. If only he could see something—anything—he would be able to tell!

He stared up at the sky blindly and twisted around, searching the darkness. Then behind him he saw a single, pale rent in the clouds. Dawn! Then he *was* conscious—the excitement, the relief of it. Mike twisted and began to swim toward the light but the spear gun fouled his legs instantly, and he went under.

As he sank down under the waves, something touched him. Despite his numbness, he felt it distinctly against his thigh—scaly and muscular and cold. The shock sobered him. He kicked convulsively to the surface.

The roughness and solidity had felt like a shark. He braced his muscles to resist the impact he thought must come. His softness and nakedness became huge in his mind, as they do under machine-gun fire. He sucked in his belly, beat with his legs in an effort to get up above the sea. He imagined the great shape of the shark below him negotiating the heaving water, waiting for a trough. A trough came. Mike dropped down into it, feeling his belly vulnerable and unprotected. He clenched his teeth, eyes, fists, toes, and waited. Another wave came, another trough; again the tension, again nothing. Mike knew that he would soon exhaust himself. He must relax; if it came, it came.

But it didn't come. He relaxed gradually, prayed for light and snatched another look at the east. The clouds were lifting off the horizon, revealing a long ingot of yellow light.

Hurry, hurry, he thought. But it didn't. It spread very slowly until the sea emerged from grayness and revealed itself fully, rolling and vast and lonely; he wished he had never seen it.

No creature rose to attack him, and gradually he got a hold on himself. He could handle the waves better now that he could see them; he could time his breathing. It was no worse than swimming in a monsoon sea, and he had had plenty of that.

He kept watching for a boat or a raft, but in all that

endless expanse, there was only him. What of the other passengers, the crew? he wondered. Surely he wasn't the only one?

Then suddenly the wind dropped. The effect was like deafness. The wind must have been diminishing for some time, and now suddenly there wasn't a breath, only the sea whishing and washing, but no spray and no thunder against his eardrums. Relief came to him and hope, and then something more arrogant—conquest. He had outlived the wind. The loneliness was back, worse than before. The sea stretched all around, endless and inescapable.

At last, the sun itself broke the ocean's rim, blazing a trail of weaving fire across the sea. The trail elongated and merged with the sky. The waves marched on Mike now in pink-gold echelons.

He felt all beaten up. Snap out of it, he thought, remembering the shark. Soon the fish would start feeding, and killer fish got very nasty in the early morning.

He got the gun unclipped and, lying with his face in the water, unstrapped the fins and mask. He got the fins on, sinking slowly down as he fitted them onto his feet. He came up quickly, very quickly, and got the snorkel mask up out of the water and peered at it blearily. The glass was intact; so was the breathing tube. The valve which kept the water out of the tube during a dive hinged freely. Thank God, he thought. He emptied the mask out, spat on the glass to stop it from clouding when he breathed, rinsed the mask out again, pulled it on and took a quick look down into the water. He did not know why he was so jumpy; there was nothing down there— only a few small shapes in the grayness. There wasn't enough light yet to see deep.

The harpoon was lashed against the barrel of the spear gun with the steel line. Lying on his face again but breathing now through the snorkel tube—interruptedly, because the high sea kept dabbing the valve shut—Mike unwound the line and got the harpoon into the projector. He wrestled with the propulsion unit for nearly a minute before he managed to compress the heavy, double spring.

As he floated to the surface and lay there, gasping weakly, he knew that that was the last time he would have the strength to do that. One shot—that was all he had.

The undersea dawned slowly beneath him. The rising sun rayed down through the plankton particles in bewildering, shifting patterns. He saw numerous fish, all fairly well down and shadowy still. It looked unbelievably deep. Something seemed to open up in his diaphragm and let the draught in. There would be fish out here he didn't know about—predatory giants as different from their reef relations as lions from alley cats.

The farther the sun got down into the water, the more fish he could see. Five, six, seven fathoms—there were fish and more fish, the deepest gleaming in the blue-blackness like sunken coins. Even as he watched, the pulse of their actions seemed to quicken. A pack of big bluefish cut into a shoal of mackerel four fathoms below him. The mackerel raced off in a tight, terrified wedge. It had started.

The whole of the visible undersea seemed to speed up like a film. The fish became no more than streaks of color in the ice-blue upper fathoms, tracing firework patterns of fear and hunger. Jacks and bonitos were everywhere, sometimes combining to tear with snapping jaws into a big shoal, then turning on one another to fight for the spoils.

The water became filled with little puffs of blood. The smell of it seemed to excite the fish to even greater ferocity and fear. This battle period lasted, normally, half an hour in the morning and the same again at nightfall. Mike wished to hell they would stop. Barracuda and sharks went crazy at feeding time; they seemed to lose all their normal fear of noise and hostile action and behaved much more in accordance with their reputation.

Suddenly three six-foot torpedolike shapes shot up out of the depths toward him. He had barely time to pull himself together before they had veered off and beaten away into the blueness. They were gun metal and silver, and shaped like gigantic mackerel—tuna. Hell, he was slow! He realized then what a sitting target he was. Lucky that was all they had been; his reflexes were all to pieces from the storm.

Almost at once another big shape appeared below him, followed by several more. They moved through the water with a sickening rush, the big one in front working its jaws like a buzz saw. They were blue shark, with pectorals like bomb fins, and paper-knife noses. Mike didn't have time to stir a muscle. They swept by underneath him, the big one spitting out fragments of fish into the water, which were snapped up by the ones behind. They were gone in an instant, and he was just letting go his breath when suddenly they were back.

It was as evil a procession as one could ever wish not to see: three pilot fish were above and slightly in front, their stripes fairly screaming danger; behind them came a ten-foot chunk of barrel-like blue muscle and, bringing up the rear, four half-grown versions of the same creature.

The sharks surged by, slamming their jaws, and disappearing into the dimness. Mike lay in the water and waited; but this time they didn't come back.

He sucked in a deep breath. It had been a matron shark airing the kids. If a plane didn't hurry up and come soon, he thought . . .

Presently, the tempo of the underwater slowed down. Breakfast was over. Mike relaxed, flattened on the surface, beating automatically with his fins, rising and falling steadily, saving his strength. The sun climbed slowly up the sky. He was really tired now, tired and thirsty. He estimated that he had been in the water for seven hours. During a full day's spearing he sometimes kept going for eight without touching down. But that was in a calm sea and in sight of land. Land, he thought longingly, with the elephants plowing the coconut groves along by the sea.

It must have been about eleven o'clock when he heard the plane. He hoisted himself as far up in the water as he could and ripped off his mask. He saw it at once. It was a biplane. It was puttering over the sea about a mile to the north, with its nose high, obviously on the lookout for something. Mike waved his mask frantically, shouted and splashed about in the water, but it kept going steadily, and eventually disappeared over the horizon.

It'll be back, he thought wildly. It's looking for the wreck. It's got to come back! He kept the mask off, forgetting the danger, forgetting everything but that up there was a fellow human being and that he must make him see him. His heart began to thump, and a great deadness spread outward from his diaphragm into his limbs.

The waves lifted and dropped him. From the crest of each he craned toward the horizon, openmouthed, hoping to hear the engine. An especially big wave heaved up in front of him. He glanced at it, gauging it automatically, then stared at it, shocked. Incased in it, as though in green ice, was a shark. It was drifting sideways in the wave, its dorsal fin lazily breaking the crest.

In a moment it would be on top of him. He threshed about with his fins to scare it, at the same time fumbling with the mask. He got it on—half filled with water—blew it out and dived.

The creature had gone. He twisted around under the water. It was behind him. It was a heavily mottled shark, seven or eight feet long. It had seen him, all right, and seemed idly curious. With a careless flick of its big tail, it nosed to within six feet of him.

Mike had one idea in mind; that was to get rid of it. Spreading his arms and legs, he hooted into the mask.

The shark's languor left it instantly. With a bewilderingly swift movement, it turned and shot away at right angles; stopped, turned and hung there, staring at Mike with its little, catlike eyes.

He cursed. These pelagic sharks weren't like the reef ones. That would have been enough even for a blackfin. He raised one ear out of the water and listened for the plane. It was coming! Its clatter reached him clearly over the waves. He took another look at the shark. Did he dare ignore it? The shark made a movement.

God! Mike thought. Not now. It can't come at me now!

But that was just what it did. He had to face it. He headed straight for it; desperation lent him strength.

Uncertainly the shark checked its advance with its pectorals. Mike kept right on, and when he was a dozen feet away from the shark he blew a burst of bubbles at it through his snorkeltube. The big mottled body jack-knifed and turned and fled, thudding the water with its tail.

Mike hit the surface and snatched off the mask all in one movement. The roar of the plane spanked his ears like a thunderclap. It was right overhead. He tried to shout, but he hadn't any air. He gasped to fill his lungs, took in some water, and choked.

The blind belly of the plane passed over him. It was an old Gladiator, with fixed undercarriage. He managed to get the gun up and wagged the duralumin in the sunlight, but the plane just pulled away steadily across the waves. He made a noise at last, something between a gasp and a scream. It just had to see him! Weird sounds dragged from his throat as he watched the machine diminish, and heard the engine grow fainter, fainter, then merge with the rush of the sea.

He was alone. He subsided, exhausted, into the waves, lying there weak and uncaring, letting the water drain into his parted mouth, letting its green weight close over him.

Oh, God, he thought. Oh, God, oh, God, oh, God.

The sun had swung over behind him and was sinking slowly toward the sea. He had been swimming since morning, weakly but steadily. After the plane, he had lain in the water a while; then some inward strength had got hold of him, turned him toward the eastern horizon, and forced his limbs to move.

Everything that was reasonable in him resisted. If another plane or a ship were to come, it would come; swimming wouldn't help. And if it didn't come the sharks would. Land, allowing the maximum for drift, was about seventy miles away, and he had never swum more than twenty in his life.

But the stubborn spirit in him did not listen. It only knew that there was land over there below the eastern rim, solid and sweet-smelling and green, and that here was only death. It drew him through the water—desperately.

His thighs were cramping a little, and he had chafe from the fins across the insteps of both feet. When they began to bleed, the sharks would pick up his trail, and yet he kept on, at intervals rolling his head up—sideways, to save energy—to look along the sea and at the sky. They were clear and empty and endless, and the light was glorious. He felt small in so much emptiness.

From his mouth and his throat right down to his stomach, he was puckered dry with brine. There wasn't a bead of moisture left in him. He wouldn't last the day. Sea creatures like Halloween masks came and went, appearing suddenly an inch from his face, then darting away. All day it had been the same, and he had let them come, grateful for their company.

Now suddenly he shortened the gun in his hand, jabbed at one with the protruding spear and transfixed it. He trapped its fin movements with his fingers, glancing round instinctively. Experience had taught him that often when you speared a fish, sharks, drawn by the sound of finny panic in the water, jumped you so fast they might have been fired at you.

He waited. Nothing happened. Without any conscious reasoning, Mike turned on his back and wrenched the fish off the barb, pushed back the mask and squeezed the lymphatic juices from its wound into his mouth. They were rank and oily and mingled with blood, but they were free from salt, and he wondered vaguely how he had known they would be.

When he had squeezed the fish dry, he threw it as far from him as possible and spiked another. He caught six; then, using his knife, cut the last one, a sea bream, into strips and ate it raw.

He felt strange and defiant, and when he sprawled back under the water, he felt no nausea but a sort of amazement. He would get stronger; he could keep alive for days like this. Then reason reasserted itself. Not without sleep, it said. His eyelids felt heavy at the thought of it. His legs stopped beating. The water was soft and warm. The movement of the waves had subsided to a soothing rhythm. His head sank.

Suddenly his eyes flicked open, and he was staring along the underglow of his own stomach. A yard from his legs was the bluish head of a shark.

He slapped the water with both fins and got himself around somehow. The solid body flicked sideways and circled lazily around him. It was more than twice his length. Then somehow there was another, rock-steady in the water and growing toward him. Mike knew he couldn't fight them. He hadn't the strength. They circled around him, puzzled by his reluctance to escape.

Mike watched them, heavy-eyed; watched a third one come—smaller, this one, with a newtlike head and dappled like a newt—a tiger shark.

There was always the gun. It was his ace, he thought, admitting to himself now what had been in the back of his mind all along. He would put it under his chin and squeeze the trigger with his bare heels.

Now, he thought. Before it's too late. The deliberate circles were narrowing steadily. He lay in the water wondering vaguely why he didn't act. There seemed to be five of them now, then six.

The undersea was darkening fast. Feeding time, he thought. They would go crazy, and it would be too late to do anything. But still he lay in the water. Deep down in him there was something that refused to die. Coward! he said angrily.

Then he was panning the gun carefully, aiming at the tiger, centering on one eye. And he knew why; it was half-grown and softer-skinned than the others, and he had to cripple it. It came in close. At seven feet he let the shark have it.

There was the sound of slithering steel and a blur and a jolt. The gun leaped out of his hand, and he was gasping air through the snorkel while the shark spun around in a tight clockwise circle. It didn't pull out of it or stop, but just tore on round and round like a Catherine wheel, and Mike knew he'd got it right in the eye.

The other sharks froze in the water; surprised, they hung there for a full moment; then they got it. All five of them hit the tiger together, rending and snapping crazily. A great cloud of blood spread in the water.

Mike dragged himself away from the scene. It was better without the gun. He swam until he couldn't go another stroke. Then he lay out in the water, panting so hard that the mask sucked in against his face with every breath.

He stared back behind him, but there was only a redness. Nothing came after him. He had played his ace.

There was no moon. The water heaved in the sultry darkness, glimmering with phosphorescence. Stars drifted above and below him. He seemed to be beating slowly through space. Darkness engulfed him; then schizopod shrimps would rise like lonely suns, thicken into constellations and drift away, and brilliant dusts would form on the undertide, then condense and flood the sea with protozoic flame. He watched his hands, leprous and white, grope through the fiery sea and traced with half-dreaming eyes the comet paths of fish. Then there was only darkness, blacker than before.

He would lift his head with an effort, into the cooler air, check with the dimmer stars for east, and hear the immeasurable sigh of the ocean. Sometimes he heard across the waves, like a gun, the sound of manta hitting the sea, and knew that somewhere nearby great thirty-foot bodies were rushing together, leaping high into the air, pressed wing tip to wing tip in their mating dance.

The Pleiades swung, and the waters gleamed and died, and once something vast and terrible rose like a city in the waves. Mike heard the water draining from its sides and saw its darkness blotting out the sea. It made a sound —something between a hiss and a moan—and presently it slid back into the depths. He heard the water sucking down after it long after it had gone.

Another sun rose, a burning eye set level with the sea. And still Mike's legs were moving, just moving. Now, he thought, now the sharks will come again, and he thought

of them as only liberators who would free him from the
instinct that tortured him on.

Again the undersea dawn began, and nothing came—
nothing but jellies, colored like sunset on ice, filling the sea
with their tilted, opening-and-closing parasols; and the
dorados, they came. With a glint of gold and greeny-blue,
they skidded into him and around him and away, kicking
up the water in bursts of saline fire. And there was blood in
the sea where the tuna caught the dorados. And still nothing came.

Mike caught a fish in his hands and ate it. He couldn't
see any sense in it, but he couldn't stop himself, either.
His legs continued to move, almost automatically, and at
high noon he saw his mother, her little-girl face collapsed
with age, and she was saying in her child-voice. "All failure is a kind of death," and he thought how right she
was. He had forgotten her failure with the old man. It
seemed to him then that they were still together and perfectly happy. He was a little crazy.

And then a shark came. It came up behind him in the
molten-metal sea, cutting through the water like the keel
of a sailing ship.

Come on, you dog, Mike said to it: You're late! Just
like the ten o'clock scholar. (He was back at school.)

He waited for it, but it wouldn't come in, just sniffed at
his fins and took a wide turn around him. He wanted it to
come in, but it wouldn't take him. Yesterday he had wanted to live, but now, he didn't care. If he could have slept,
he would have been all right, but now he just wanted the
shark to hurry up and get it over with.

So he turned his back, and when he looked round
again the shark was gone. It stayed gone, and the sun
burned down on the sea, which became like watered silk,
very glossy and silent, and the sound he made blowing
through the snorkel seemed to grow very loud, like the
roaring of the locomotives in Bay St. Louis station. He
relaxed into a kind of dream, and he was back in the old
city, in the old apartment, dirty from working at the garage. The old man was there, and Mike had just said he

couldn't stick it any more with Mum gone and everything shot to pieces the way it was—that he was heading for the Far East, Ceylon maybe. His old man looked up at him over the tops of his glasses, with his mouth turned down and his eyes preoccupied with other people and other places, and seeing him like that, Mike suddenly realized that he really was an old man.

Then the sun drowned in a sea of blood, and he was alone in the dusk with night moving up the sky. This was his last night, he thought. Tonight he would die. There was nothing left in him to regret with or to pray with, nothing but this instinct driving him on with limbs he could no longer feel.

At last the sharks came. They came with the departing light, like slim blades in the sea. There was nothing to stop them, but they came on carefully, avoiding his fire-trail in the darkening water. He closed his eyes. It was getting late.

The sunset's imprisoned image burned dimly in his brain, like a candle guttering low, and sounds grew enormous in the water. For an instant, poised on the edge of delirium, he heard the whisper of his own fins and, behind them, the shudder of tails, like someone thrumming the deadened bass string of a harp with their fingernails. The tempo increased. Now, he thought. At last! The water shook against him, beat on his eardrums, diminished and was still.

His lids flickered. Below, in the iridescence, fish-trails sparkled through the water like a million shooting stars. They streaked ahead of him and were gone; then more in gleaming panic, raced by—then more and more.

There was thunder in the sea, but he didn't hear it. He fell into a dreamy state. It seemed to him that the waters were boiling around him with phosphorescent light; that he was lifted and flung, buffeted by tails, flung again; that in the luminosity he saw the ocean packed solid with gleaming backs, heard their panting and heaving. Then he was down under the water, and the migrating false killer whales were above him, lighted by the phosphorescence, belly upon belly, rank upon rank.

Then somehow there was air and the sea eddied and gleamed, and the turmoil rumbled away across the sea, and he was alone.

A light forced its way under his lids, and he turned away from it. There were cold bodies around him, and when he moved they squirmed. It was still a dream, and it was wrong somehow that there should be a man in it, holding a lamp, and, in the dimness, others staring at him.

They wore ragged sarongs, and they looked for all the world like Singhalese fishermen. For some reason their eyes were wide and frightened. Their hands were dragging at a net; Mike realized suddenly that he was in the net—caught!

He learned later that he had wound up a mile off Galle, South Ceylon. He never knew how; probably the current had been working with him all the way. But somehow he had made it. The fishermen admitted afterward that they had thought he was some strange kind of monster and had nearly lit into him with their gaffs. The incident certainly gave rise to some queer tales which Mike didn't altogether like. The Ceylon *Courier* gave him a full-page spread. "Fish-man," the article called him again and again, and when he got out of the hospital and went down into Colombo, people looked at him strangely and weren't quite sure what to do with their eyes when they talked to him. He never spoke about it much himself, because of the feeling he had had in the net.

He knew it was a net and that they were men around him—and he was afraid. The lamp seemed to draw his eyes till the flame filled his mind, and in the darkness all around, there was terror. He gasped for air, but none would come. He struggled, and the other fish around him struggled, and he twisted and kicked, knowing only that he must get back to the sea, that he must slither back somehow into the dark cavern of the water and dart away through the softness and the silence to where he belonged. It was a sensation of the purest fear—uninhibited by logic or pride or anything human, undiluted and nightmarish—such as only a wild creature might feel when it falls a victim to man.

Then one of the natives bent over him and took off his fouled-up mask, and there was air in a cool rush and he blacked out.

RIKKI-TIKKI-TAVI

by Rudyard Kipling

At the hole where he went in
    Red-Eye called to Wrinkle-Skin.
Hear what little Red-Eye saith:
"Nag, come up and dance with death!"

Eye to eye and head to head,
    (*Keep the measure, Nag.*)
This shall end when one is dead;
    (*At thy pleasure, Nag.*)

Turn for turn and twist for twist—
    (*Run and hide thee, Nag.*)
Hah! The hooded Death has missed!
    (*Woe betide thee, Nag!*)

THIS IS THE STORY of the great war that Rikki-tikki-tavi fought single-handed, through the bathrooms of the big bungalow in Segowlee cantonment. Darzee, the tailor-bird, helped him, and Chuchundra, the muskrat, who never comes out into the middle of the floor, but always creeps round by the wall, gave him advice; but Rikki-tikki did the real fighting.

He was a mongoose, rather like a little cat in his fur and his tail, but quite like a weasel in his head and his habits. His eyes and the end of his restless nose were pink; he could scratch himself anywhere he pleased, with any leg, front or back, that he chose to use; he could fluff up his tail till it looked like a bottle-brush, and his war-cry as he scuttled through the long grass, was: "*Rikk-tikk-tikki-tikki-tchk!*"

One day, a high summer flood washed him out of the burrow where he lived with his father and mother, and carried him, kicking and clucking, down a roadside ditch. He found a little wisp of grass floating there, and clung to it till he lost his senses. When he revived, he was lying in the hot sun on the middle of a garden path, very draggled indeed, and a small boy was saying: "Here's a dead mongoose. Let's have a funeral."

"No," said his mother; "let's take him in and dry him. Perhaps he isn't really dead."

They took him into the house, and a big man picked him up between his fingers and thumb and said he was not dead but half choked; so they wrapped him in cotton-wool, and warmed him, and he opened his eyes and sneezed.

"Now," said the big man (he was an Englishman who had just moved into the bungalow); "don't frighten him, and we'll see what he'll do."

It is the hardest thing in the world to frighten a mongoose, because he is eaten up from nose to tail with curiosity. The motto of all the mongoose family is, "Run and find out"; and Rikki-tikki was a true mongoose. He looked at the cotton-wool, decided that it was not good to eat, ran all round the table, sat up and put his fur in order, scratched himself, and jumped on the small boy's shoulder.

"Don't be frightened, Teddy," said his father. "That's his way of making friends."

"Ouch! He's tickling under my chin," said Teddy.

Rikki-tikki looked down between the boy's collar and neck, snuffed at his ear, and climbed down to the floor, where he sat rubbing his nose.

"Good gracious," said Teddy's mother, "and that's a wild creature! I suppose he's so tame because we've been kind to him."

"All mongooses are like that," said her husband. "If Teddy doesn't pick him up by the tail, or try to put him in a cage, he'll run in and out of the house all day long. Let's give him something to eat."

They gave him a little piece of raw meat. Rikki-tikki

liked it immensely, and when it was finished he went out into the veranda and sat in the sunshine and fluffed up his fur to make it dry to the roots. Then he felt better.

"There are more things to find out about in this house," he said to himself, "than all my family could find out in all their lives. I shall certainly stay and find out."

He spent all that day roaming over the house. He nearly drowned himself in the bath-tubs, put his nose into the ink on a writing-table, and burned it on the end of the big man's cigar, for he climbed up in the big man's lap to see how writing was done. At nightfall he ran into Teddy's nursery to watch how kerosene lamps were lighted, and when Teddy went to bed Rikki-tikki climbed up too; but he was a restless companion, because he had to get up and attend to every noise all through the night, and find out what made it. Teddy's mother and father came in, the last thing, to look at their boy, and Rikki-tikki was awake on the pillow. "I don't like that," said Teddy's mother; "he may bite the child." "He'll do no such thing," said the father. "Teddy's safer with that little beast than if he had a bloodhound to watch him. If a snake came into the nursery now——"

But Teddy's mother wouldn't think of anything so awful.

Early in the morning Rikki-tikki came to early breakfast in the veranda riding on Teddy's shoulder, and they gave him banana and some boiled egg; and he sat on all their laps one after the other, because every well-brought-up mongoose always hopes to be a house-mongoose some day and have rooms to run about in, and Rikki-tikki's mother (she used to live in the General's house at Segowlee) had carefully told Rikki what to do if ever he came across white men.

Then Rikki-tikki went out into the garden to see what was to be seen. It was a large garden, only half cultivated, with bushes as big as summer-houses of Marshal Niel roses, lime and orange trees, clumps of bamboo, and thickets of high grass. Rikki-tikki licked his lips. "This is a splendid hunting-ground," he said, and his tail grew bottle-brushy at the thought of it, and he scuttled up and down the garden, snuffing here and there till he heard very sorrowful voices in a thorn-bush.

It was Darzee, the tailor-bird, and his wife. They had made a beautiful nest by pulling two big leaves together and stitching them up the edges with fibers, and had filled the hollow with cotton and downy fluff. The nest swayed to and fro, as they sat on the rim and cried.

"What is the matter?" asked Rikki-tikki.

"We are very miserable," said Darzee. "One of our babies fell out of the nest yesterday and Nag ate him."

"H'm!" said Rikki-tikki, "that is very sad—but I am a stranger here. Who is Nag?"

Darzee and his wife only cowered down in the nest without answering, for from the thick grass at the foot of the bush there came a low hiss—a horrid cold sound that made Rikki-tikki jump back two clear feet. Then inch by inch out of the grass rose up the head and spread hood of Nag, the big black cobra, and he was five feet long from tongue to tail. When he had lifted one-third of himself clear of the ground, he stayed balancing to and fro exactly as a dandelion-tuft balances in the wind, and he looked at Rikki-tikki with the wicked snake's eyes that never change their expression, whatever the snake may be thinking of.

"Who is Nag?" he said. "*I* am Nag. The great god Brahm put his mark upon all our people when the first cobra spread his hood to keep the sun off Brahm as he slept. Look, and be afraid!"

He spread out his hood more than ever, and Rikki-tikki saw the spectacle-mark on the back of it that looks exactly like the eye part of a hook-and-eye fastening. He was afraid for the minute; but it is impossible for a mongoose to stay frightened for any length of time, and though Rikki-tikki had never met a live cobra before, his mother had fed him on dead ones, and he knew that all a grown mongoose's business in life was to fight and eat snakes. Nag knew that too, and at the bottom of his cold heart he was afraid.

"Well," said Rikki-tikki, and his tail began to fluff up

again, "marks or no marks, do you think it is right for you to eat fledglings out of a nest?"

Nag was thinking to himself, and watching the least little movement in the grass behind Rikki-tikki. He knew that mongooses in the garden meant death sooner or later for him and his family; but he wanted to get Rikki-tikki off his guard. So he dropped his head a little, and put it on one side.

"Let us talk," he said. "You eat eggs. Why should not I eat birds?"

"Behind you! Look behind you!" sang Darzee.

Rikki-tikki knew better than to waste time in staring. He jumped up in the air as high as he could go, and just under him whizzed by the head of Nagaina, Nag's wicked wife. She had crept up behind him as he was talking, to make an end of him; and he heard her savage hiss as the stroke missed. He came down almost across her back, and if he had been an old mongoose he would have known that then was the time to break her back with one bite; but he was afraid of the terrible lashing return-stroke of the cobra. He bit, indeed, but did not bite long enough, and he jumped clear of the whisking tail, leaving Nagaina torn and angry.

"Wicked, wicked Darzee!" said Nag, lashing up as high as he could reach toward the nest in the thorn-bush; but Darzee had built it out of reach of snakes, and it only swayed to and fro.

Rikki-tikki felt his eyes growing red and hot (when a mongoose's eyes grow red, he is angry), and he sat back on his tail and hind legs like a little kangaroo, and looked all around him, and chattered with rage. But Nag and Nagaina had disappeared into the grass. When a snake misses its stroke, it never says anything or gives any sign of what it means to do next. Rikki-tikki did not care to follow them, for he did not feel sure that he could manage two snakes at once. So he trotted off to the gravel path near the house, and sat down to think. It was a serious matter for him.

If you read the old books of natural history, you will find they say that when the mongoose fights the snake and happens to get bitten, he runs off and eats some herb that cures him. That is not true. The victory is only a matter of quickness of eye and quickness of foot,—snake's blow against mongoose's jump,—and as no eye can follow the motion of a snake's head when it strikes, that makes things much more wonderful than any magic herb. Rikki-tikki knew he was a young mongoose, and it made him all the more pleased to think he had managed to escape a blow from behind. It gave him confidence in himself and when Teddy came running down the path, Rikki-tikki was ready to be petted.

But just as Teddy was stopping, something flinched a little in the dust, and a tiny voice said: "Be careful. I am death!" It was Karait, the dusty brown snakeling that lies for choice on the dusty earth; and his bite is as dangerous as the cobra's. But he is so small that nobody thinks of him, and so he does the more harm to people.

Rikki-tikki's eyes grew red again, and he danced up to Karait with the peculiar rocking, swaying motion that he had inherited from his family. It looks very funny, but it is so perfectly balanced a gait that you can fly off from it at any angle you please; and in dealing with snakes this is an advantage. If Rikki-tikki had only known, he was doing a much more dangerous thing than fighting Nag for Karait is so small, and can turn so quickly, that unless Rikki bit him close to the back of the head, he would get the return-stroke in his eye or lip. But Rikki did not know: his eyes were all red, and he rocked back and forth, looking for a good place to hold. Karait struck out. Rikki jumped sideways and tried to run in, but the wicked little dusty gray head lashed within a fraction of his shoulder, and he had to jump over the body, and the head followed his heels close.

Teddy shouted to the house: "Oh, look here! Our mongoose is killing a snake"; and Rikki-tikki heard a scream from Teddy's mother. His father ran out with a stick, but by the time he came up, Karait had lunged out once too far, and Rikki-tikki had sprung, jumped on the snake's back, dropped his head far between his fore legs, bitten as high up the back as he could get hold, and rolled away. That bite paralyzed Karait, and Rikki-tikki was just going to eat him up from the tail, after the custom of his family at dinner, when he remembered that a full meal makes a slow mongoose, and if he wanted all his strength and quickness ready, he must keep himself thin.

He went away for a dust-bath under the castor-oil bushes, while Teddy's father beat the dead Karait. "What is the use of that?" thought Rikki-tikki. "I have settled it all"; and then Teddy's mother picked him up from the dust and hugged him, crying that he had saved Teddy from death, and Teddy's father said that he was a providence, and Teddy looked on with big scared eyes. Rikki-tikki was rather amused, at all the fuss, which, of course, he did not understand. Teddy's mother might just as well have petted Teddy for playing in the dust. Rikki was thoroughly enjoying himself.

That night, at dinner, walking to and fro among the wine-glasses on the table, he could have stuffed himself three times over with nice things; but he remembered Nag and Nagaina, and though it was very pleasant to be patted and petted by Teddy's mother and to sit on Teddy's shoulders, his eyes would get red from time to time, and he would go off into his long war-cry of *"Rikk-tikk-tik-ki-tikki-tchk!"*

Teddy carried him off to bed, and insisted on Rikki-tikki sleeping under his chin. Rikki-tikki was too well bred to bite or scratch, but as soon as Teddy was asleep he went off for his nightly walk around the house, and in the dark he ran up against Chuchundra, the muskrat, creeping round by the wall. Chuchundra is a broken-hearted little beast. He whimpers and cheeps all the night, trying to make up his mind to run into the middle of the room, but he never gets there.

"Don't kill me," said Chuchundra, almost weeping. "Rikki-tikki, don't kill me."

"Do you think a snake-killer kills muskrats?" said Rikki-tikki scornfully.

"Those who kill snakes get killed by snakes," said Chuchundra, more sorrowfully than ever. "And how am I to be sure that Nag won't mistake me for you some dark night?"

"There's not the least danger," said Rikki-tikki; "but Nag is in the garden, and I know you don't go there."

"My cousin Chua, the rat, told me—" said Chuchundra, and then he stopped.

"Told you what?"

"H'sh! Nag is everywhere, Rikki-tikki. You should have talked to Chua in the garden."

"I didn't—so you must tell me. Quick Chuchundra, or I'll bite you!"

Chuchundra sat down and cried till the tears rolled off his whiskers. "I am a very poor man," he sobbed. "I never had spirit enough to run out into the middle of the room. H'sh! I mustn't tell you anything. Can't you *hear*, Rikki-tikki?"

Rikki-tikki listened. The house was as still as still, but he thought he could just catch the faintest *scratch-scratch* in the world,—a noise as faint as that of a wasp walking on a window-pane,—the dry scratch of snake's scales on brickwork.

"That's Nag or Nagaina," he said to himself; "and he is crawling into the bath-room sluice. You're right, Chuchundra; I should have talked to Chua."

He stole off to Teddy's bath-room, but there was nothing there, and then to Teddy's mother's bath-room. At the bottom of the smooth plaster wall there was a brick pulled out to make a sluice for the bath-water, and as Rikki-tikki stole in by the masonry curb where the bath is put, he heard Nag and Nagaina whispering together outside in the moonlight.

"When the house is emptied of people," said Nagaina to her husband, *"he* will have to go away, and then the garden will be our own again. Go in quietly, and remember that the big man who killed Karait is the first one to bite. Then come out and tell me, and we will hunt for Rikki-tikki together."

"But are you sure that there is anything to be gained by killing the people?" said Nag.

"Everything. When there were no people in the bungalow, did we have any mongoose in the garden? So long as the bungalow is empty, we are king and queen of the garden; and remember that as soon as our eggs in the melon-bed hatch (as they may tomorrow), our children will need room and quiet."

"I had not thought of that," said Nag. "I will go, but there is no need that we should hunt for Rikki-tikki afterward. I will kill the big man and his wife, and the child if I can, and come away quietly. Then the bungalow will be empty, and Rikki-tikki will go."

Rikki-tikki tingled all over with rage and hatred at this, and then Nag's head came through the sluice, and his five feet of cold body followed it. Angry as he was, Rikki-tikki was very frightened as he saw the size of the big cobra. Nag coiled himself up, raised his head, and looked into the bath-room in the dark, and Rikki could see his eyes glitter.

"Now, if I kill him here, Nagaina will know; and if I fight him on the open floor, the odds are in his favour. What am I to do?" said Rikki-tikki-tavi.

Nag waved to and fro, and then Rikki-tikki heard him drinking from the biggest water-jar that was used to fill the bath. "That is good," said the snake. "Now, when Karait was killed, the big man had a stick. He may have that stick still, but when he comes in to bathe in the morning he will not have a stick. I shall wait here till he comes. Nagaina—do you hear me?—I shall wait here in the cool till daytime."

There was no answer from outside, so Rikki-tikki knew Nagaina had gone away. Nag coiled himself down, coil by coil, round the bulge at the bottom of the water-jar, and Rikki-tikki stayed still as death. After an hour he began to move, muscle by muscle, toward the jar. Nag was asleep, and Rikki-tikki looked at his big back, wondering which would be the best place for a good hold. "If I don't break his back at the first jump," said Rikki, "he still can fight; and if he fights—O Rikki!" He looked at the thickness of the neck below the hood, but that was too much for him; and a bite near the tail would only make Nag savage.

"It must be the head," he said at last; "the head above the hood; and, when I am once there, I must not let go."

Then he jumped. The head was lying a little clear of the water-jar, under the curve of it; and, as his teeth met, Rikki braced his back against the bulge of the red earthenware to hold down the head. This gave him just one second's purchase, and he made the most of it. Then he was battered to and fro as a rat is shaken by a dog—to and fro on the floor, up and down, and round in great circles; but his eyes were red, and he held on as the body cartwhipped over the floor, upsetting the tin dipper and the soap-dish and the flesh-brush, and banged against the tin side of the bath. As he held he closed his jaws tighter and tighter, for he made sure he would be banged to death, and, for the honour of his family, he preferred to be found with his teeth locked. He was dizzy, aching, and felt shaken to pieces when something went off like a thunderclap just behind him; a hot wind knocked him senseless and red fire singed his fur. The big man had been wakened by the noise, and had fired both barrels of a shot-gun into Nag just behind the hood.

Rikki-tikki held on with his eyes shut, for now he was quite sure he was dead; but the head did not move, and the big man picked him up and said: "It's the mongoose again, Alice; the little chap has saved *our* lives now." Then Teddy's mother came in with a very white face, and saw what was left of Nag, and Rikki-tikki dragged himself to Teddy's bedroom and spent half the rest of the night shaking himself tenderly to find out whether he really was broken into forty pieces, as he fancied.

When morning came he was very stiff, but well pleased with his doings. "Now I have Nagaina to settle with, and she will be worse than five Nags, and there's no knowing when the eggs she spoke of will hatch. Goodness! I must go and see Darzee," he said.

Without waiting for breakfast, Rikki-tikki ran to the thorn-bush where Darzee was singing a song of triumph at the top of his voice. The news of Nag's death was all over the garden, for the sweeper had thrown the body on the rubbish-heap.

"Oh, you stupid tuft of feathers!" said Rikki-tikki, angrily. "Is this the time to sing?"

"Nag is dead—is dead—is dead!" sang Darzee. "The valiant Rikki-tikki caught him by the head and held fast. The big man brought the bang-stick and Nag fell in two pieces! He will never eat my babies again."

"All that's true enough; but where's Nagaina?" said Rikki-tikki, looking carefully round him.

"Nagaina came to the bath-room sluice and called for Nag," Darzee went on; "and Nag came out on the end of a stick—the sweeper picked him up on the end of a stick and threw him upon the rubbish-heap. Let us sing about the great, the red-eyed Rikki-tikki!" and Darzee filled his throat and sang.

"If I could get up to your nest, I'd roll all your babies out!" said Rikki-tikki. "You don't know when to do the right thing at the right time. You're safe enough in your nest there, but it's war for me down here. Stop singing a minute, Darzee."

"For the great, the beautiful Rikki-tikki's sake I will stop," said Darzee. "What is it, O Killer of the terrible Nag?"

"Where is Nagaina, for the third time?"

"On the rubbish-heap by the stables, mourning for Nag. Great is Rikki-tikki with the white teeth."

"Bother my white teeth! Have you ever heard where she keeps her eggs?"

"In the melon-bed, on the end nearest the wall, where the sun strikes nearly all day. She had them there weeks ago."

"And you never thought it worth while to tell me? The end nearest the wall, you said?"

"Rikki-tikki, you are not going to eat her eggs?"

"Not eat exactly; no. Darzee, if you have a grain of sense you will fly off to the stables and pretend that your wing is broken, and let Nagaina chase you away to this bush! I must get to the melon-bed, and if I went there now she'd see me."

Darzee was a feather-brained little fellow who could never hold more than one idea at a time in his head; and just because he knew that Nagaina's children were born in eggs like his own, he didn't think at first that it was fair to kill them. But his wife was a sensible bird, and she knew that cobra's eggs meant young cobras later on; so she flew off from the nest, and left Darzee to keep the babies warm, and continue his song about the death of Nag. Darzee was very like a man in some ways.

She fluttered in front of Nagaina by the rubbish-heap, and cried out, "Oh, my wing is broken! The boy in the house threw a stone at me and broke it." Then she fluttered more desperately than ever.

Nagaina lifted up her head and hissed, "You warned Rikki-tikki when I would have killed him. Indeed and truly, you've chosen a bad place to be lame in." And she moved toward Darzee's wife, slipping along over the dust.

"The boy broke it with a stone!" shrieked Darzee's wife.

"Well! It may be some consolation to you when you're dead to know that I shall settle accounts with the boy. My husband lies on the rubbish-heap this morning, but before night the boy in the house will lie very still. What is the use of running away? I am sure to catch you. Little fool, look at me!"

Darzee's wife knew better than to do *that,* for a bird who looks at a snake's eyes gets so frightened that she cannot move. Darzee's wife fluttered on, piping sorrowfully, and never leaving the ground, and Nagaina quickened her pace.

Rikki-tikki heard them going up the path from the stables, and he raced for the end of the melon-patch near the wall. There, in the warm litter about the melons, very cunningly hidden, he found twenty-five eggs, about the size of a bantam's eggs, but with whitish skin instead of shell.

"I was not a day too soon," he said; for he could see the baby cobras curled up inside the skin, and he knew that the minute they were hatched they could each kill a man or a mongoose. He bit off the tops of the eggs as fast as he could, taking care to crush the young cobras, and turned over the litter from time to time to see whether he had missed any. At last there were only three eggs left, and Rikki-tikki began to chuckle to himself, when he heard Darzee's wife screaming.

"Rikki-tikki, I led Nagaina toward the house, and she has gone into the veranda, and—oh, come quickly—she means killing!"

Rikki-tikki smashed two eggs, and tumbled backward down the melon-bed with the third egg in his mouth, and scuttled to the veranda as hard as he could put foot to the ground. Teddy and his mother and father were there at early breakfast; but Rikki-tikki saw that they were not eating anything. They sat stone-still, and their faces were white. Nagaina was coiled up on the matting by Teddy's chair, within easy striking distance of Teddy's bare leg, and she was swaying to and fro singing a song of triumph.

"Son of the big man that killed Nag," she hissed, "stay still. I am not ready yet. Wait a little. Keep very still, all you three. If you move I strike, and if you do not move I strike. Oh, foolish people, who killed my Nag!"

Teddy's eyes were fixed on his father, and all his father could do was to whisper, "Sit still, Teddy. You mustn't move. Teddy, keep still."

Then Rikki-tikki came up and cried: "Turn round, Nagaina; turn and fight!"

"All in good time," said she, without moving her eyes. "I will settle my account with *you* presently. Look at your friends, Rikki-tikki. They are still and white; they are afraid. They dare not move, and if you come a step nearer I strike."

"Look at your eggs," said Rikki-tikki, "in the melon-bed near the wall. Go and look, Nagaina."

The big snake turned half round, and saw the egg on the veranda. "Ah-h! Give it to me," she said.

Tikki-tikki put his paws one on each side of the egg, and his eyes were blood-red. "What price for a snake's egg? For a young cobra? For a young king-cobra? For the last—the very last of the brood? The ants are eating all the others down by the melon-bed."

Nagaina spun clear round, forgetting everything for the sake of the one egg; and Rikki-tikki saw Teddy's father shoot out a big hand, catch Teddy by the shoulder and drag him across the little table with the tea-cups, safe and out of reach of Nagaina.

"Tricked! Tricked! Tricked! *Rikk-tck-tck!*" chuckled Rikki-tikki. "The boy is safe, and it was I—I—I that caught Nag by the hood last night in the bath-room." Then he began to jump up and down, all four feet together, his head close to the floor. "He threw me to and fro, but he could not shake me off. He was dead before the big man blew him in two. I did it. *Rikki-tikki-tck-tck!* Come then, Nagaina. Come and fight with me. You shall not be a widow long."

Nagaina saw that she had lost her chance of killing Teddy, and the egg lay between Rikki-tikki's paws. "Give me the egg, Rikki-tikki. Give me the last of my eggs, and I will go away and never come back," she said, lowering her hood.

"Yes, you will go away, and you will never come back; for you will go to the rubbish-heap with Nag. Fight, widow! The big man has gone for his gun! Fight!"

Rikki-tikki was bounding all round Nagaina, keeping just out of the reach of her stroke, his little eyes like hot coals. Nagaina gathered herself together, and flung out at him. Rikki-tikki jumped up and backward. Again and again and again she struck, and each time her head came with a whack on the matting of the veranda and she gathered herself together like a watch-spring. Then Rikki-tikki danced in a circle to get behind her, and Nagaina spun round to keep her head to his head, so that the rustle of her tail on the matting sounded like dry leaves blown along by the wind.

He had forgotten the egg. It still lay on the veranda, and Nagaina came nearer and nearer to it, till at last, while Rikki-tikki was drawing breath, she caught it in her mouth, turned to the veranda steps, and flew like an arrow down the path, with Rikki-tikki behind her. When the cobra runs for her life, she goes like a whip-lash flicked across a horse's neck.

Rikki-tikki knew that he must catch her, or all the trouble would begin again. She headed straight for the long grass by the thorn-bush, and as he was running Rikki-tikki heard Darzee still singing his foolish little song of triumph. But Darzee's wife was wiser. She flew off her nest as Nagaina came along, and flapped her wings about Nagaina's head. If Darzee had helped they might have turned her; but Nagaina only lowered her hood and went on. Still, the instant's delay brought Rikki-tikki up to her, and as she plunged into the rat-hole where she and Nag used to live, his little white teeth were clenched on her tail, and he went down with her—and very few mongooses, however wise and old they may be, care to follow a cobra into its hole. It was dark in the hole; and Rikki-tikki never knew when it might open out and give Nagaina room to turn and strike at him. He held on savagely, and struck out his feet to act as brakes on the dark slope of the hot, moist earth.

Then the grass by the mouth of the hole stopped waving, and Darzee said: "It is all over with Rikki-tikki! We must sing his death-song. Valiant Rikki-tikki is dead! For Nagaina will surely kill him underground."

So he sang a very mournful song that he made up all on the spur of the minute, and just as he got to the most touching part the grass quivered again, and Rikki-tikki, covered with dirt, dragged himself out of the hole leg by leg, licking his whiskers. Darzee stopped with a little shout. Rikki-tikki shook some of the dust out of his fur and sneezed. "It is all over," he said. "The widow will never come out again." And the red ants that live between the grass stems heard him, and began to troop down one after another to see if he had spoken the truth.

Rikki-tikki curled himself up in the grass and slept where he was—slept and slept till it was late in the afternoon, for he had done a hard day's work.

"Now," he said, when he awoke, "I will go back to the house. Tell the Coppersmith, Darzee, and he will tell the garden that Nagaina is dead."

The Coppersmith is a bird who makes a noise exactly like the beating of a little hammer on a copper pot; and the reason he is always making it is because he is the towncrier to every Indian garden, and tells all the news to everybody who cares to listen. As Rikki-tikki went up the path, he heard his "attention" notes like a tiny dinner-gong; and then the steady *"Ding-dong-tock!* Nag is dead —*dong!* Nagaina is dead! *Ding-dong-tock!"* That set all the birds in the garden singing, and the frogs croaking; for Nag and Nagaina used to eat frogs as well as little birds.

When Rikki got to the house, Teddy and Teddy's mother (she looked very white still, for she had been fainting) and Teddy's father came out and almost cried over him; and that night he ate all that was given him till he could eat no more, and went to bed on Teddy's shoulder, where Teddy's mother saw him when she came to look late at night.

"He saved our lives and Teddy's life," she said to her husband. "Just think, he saved all our lives."

Rikki-tikki woke up with a jump, for all the mongooses are light sleepers.

"Oh, it's you," said he. "What are you bothering for? All the cobras are dead; and if they weren't I'm here."

Rikki-tikki had a right to be proud of himself; but he did not grow too proud, and he kept that garden as a mongoose should keep it, with tooth and jump and spring and bite, till never a cobra dared show its head inside the walls.

DARZEE'S CHAUNT

(SUNG IN HONOUR OF RIKKI-TIKKI-TAVI)

Singer and tailor am I—
   Doubled the joys that I know—
Proud of my lilt through the sky,
   Proud of the house that I sew—
Over and under, so weave I my music—so weave I the house
   that I sew.

Sing to your fledgings again,
   Mother, oh lift up your head!
Evil that plagued us is slain,
   Death in the garden lies dead.
Terror that hid in the roses is impotent—flung on the dung-
   hill and dead!

Who hath delivered us, who?
Tell me his nest and his name.
Rikki, the valiant, the true,
Tikki, with eyeballs of flame.
Rik-tikki-tikki, the ivory-fanged, the hunter with eyeballs of
flame.

Give him the Thanks of the Birds,
Bowing with tail-feathers spread!
Praise him with nightingale words–
Nay, I will praise him instead.
Hear! I will sing you the praise of the bottle-tailed Rikki,
with eyeballs of red!

(Here Rikki-tikki interrupted, and the rest of the song is lost.)

TO BUILD A FIRE

by Jack London

DAY HAD BROKEN cold and grey, exceedingly cold and grey, when the man turned aside from the main Yukon trail and climbed the high earth-bank, where a dim and little-travelled trail led eastward through the fat spruce timberland. It was a steep bank, and he paused for breath at the top, excusing the act to himself by looking at his watch. It was nine o'clock. There was no sun nor hint of sun, though there was not a cloud in the sky. It was a clear day, and yet there seemed an intangible pall over the face of things, a subtle gloom that made the day dark, and that was due to the absence of sun. This fact did not worry the man. He was used to the lack of sun. It had been days since he had seen the sun, and he knew that a few more days must pass before that cheerful orb, due south, would just peep above the sky-line and dip immediately from view.

The man flung a look back along the way he had come. The Yukon lay a mile wide and hidden under three feet of ice. On top of this ice were as many feet of snow. It was all pure white, rolling in gentle undulations where the ice-jams of the freeze-up had formed. North and south, as far as his eye could see, it was unbroken white, save for a dark hair-line that curved and twisted from around the spruce-covered island to the south, and that curved and twisted away into the north, where it disappeared behind another spruce-covered island. This dark hair-line was the trail—the main trail—that led south five hundred miles to the Chilcoot Pass, Dyea, and salt water;

and that led north seventy miles to Dawson, and still on to the north a thousand miles to Nulato, and finally to St. Michael on Bering Sea, a thousand miles and half a thousand more.

But all this—the mysterious, far-reaching hair-line trail, the absence of sun from the sky, the tremendous cold, and the strangeness and weirdness of it all—made no impression on the man. It was not because he was long used to it. He was a newcomer in the land, a *chechaquo,* and this was his first winter. The trouble with him was that he was without imagination. He was quick and alert in the things of life, but only in the things, and not in the significances. Fifty degrees below zero meant eighty-odd degrees of frost. Such fact impressed him as being cold and uncomfortable, and that was all. It did not lead him to meditate upon his frailty as a creature of temperature, and upon man's frailty in general, able only to live within certain narrow limits of heat and cold; and from there on it did not lead him to the conjectural field of immortality and man's place in the universe. Fifty degrees below zero stood for a bite of frost that hurt and that must be guarded against by the use of mittens, earflaps, warm moccasins, and thick socks. Fifty degrees below zero was to him just precisely fifty degrees below zero. That there should be anything more to it than that was a thought that never entered his head.

As he turned to go on, he spat speculatively. There was a sharp, explosive crackle that startled him. He spat again. And again, in the air, before it could fall to the snow, the spittle crackled. He knew that at fifty below spittle crackled on the snow, but this spittle had crackled in the air. Undoubtedly it was colder than fifty below—how much colder he did not know. But the temperature did not matter. He was bound for the old claim on the left fork of Henderson Creek, where the boys were already. They had come over across the divide from the Indian Creek country, while he had come the roundabout way to take a look at the possibilities of getting out logs in the spring from the islands in the Yukon. He would be in to camp by six o'clock; a bit after dark, it was true, but the boys would be there, a fire would be going, and a hot supper would be ready. As for lunch, he pressed his hand against the protruding bundle under his jacket. It was also under his shirt, wrapped up in a handkerchief and lying against the naked skin. It was the only way to keep the biscuits from freezing. He smiled agreeably to himself as he thought of those biscuits, each cut open and sopped in bacon grease, and each enclosing a generous slice of fried bacon.

He plunged in among the big spruce trees. The trail was faint. A foot of snow had fallen since the last sled had passed over, and he was glad he was without a sled, travelling light. In fact, he carried nothing but the lunch wrapped in the handkerchief. He was surprised, however, at the cold. It certainly was cold, he concluded, as he rubbed his numb nose and cheekbones with his mittened hand. He was a warm-whiskered man, but the hair on his face did not protect the high cheek-bones and the eager nose that thrust itself aggressively into the frosty air.

At the man's heels trotted a dog, a big native husky, the proper wolf-dog, grey-coated and without any visible or temperamental difference from its brother, the wild wolf. The animal was depressed by the tremendous cold. It knew that it was no time for travelling. Its instinct told it a truer tale than was told to the man by the man's judgment. In reality, it was not merely colder than fifty below zero; it was colder than sixty below, than seventy below. It was seventy-five below zero. Since the freezing-point is thirty-two above zero, it meant that one hundred and seven degrees of frost obtained. The dog did not know anything about thermometers. Possibly in its brain there was no sharp consciousness of a condition of very cold such as was in the man's brain. But the brute had its instinct. It experienced a vague but menacing apprehension that subdued it and made it slink along at the man's heels, and that made it question eagerly every unwonted movement of the man as if expecting him to go into camp or to seek shelter somewhere and build a fire. The dog had learned fire, and it wanted fire, or else to burrow under the snow and cuddle its warmth away from the air.

The frozen moisture of its breathing had settled on its fur in a fine powder of frost, and especially were its jowls, muzzle, and eyelashes whitened by its crystalled breath. The man's red beard and mustache were likewise frosted, but more solidly, the deposit taking the form of ice and increasing with every warm, moist breath he exhaled. Also, the man was chewing tobacco, and the muzzle of ice held his lips so rigidly that he was unable to clear his chin when he expelled the juice. The result was that a crystal beard of the color and solidity of amber was increasing its length on his chin. If he fell down it would shatter itself, like glass, into brittle fragments. But he did not mind the appendage. It was the penalty all tobacco-chewers paid in that country, and he had been out before in two cold snaps. They had not been so cold as this, he knew, but by the spirit thermometer at Sixty Mile he knew they had been registered at fifty below and at fifty-five.

He held on through the level stretch of woods for several miles, crossed a wide flat of nigger-heads, and dropped down a bank to the frozen bed of a small stream. This was Henderson Creek, and he knew he was ten miles from the forks. He looked at his watch. It was ten o'clock. He was making four miles an hour, and he calculated that that he would arrive at the forks at half-past twelve. He decided to celebrate that event by eating his lunch there.

The dog dropped in again at his heels, with a tail drooping discouragement, as the man swung along the creekbed. The furrow of the old sled-trail was plainly visible, but a dozen inches of snow covered the marks of the last runners. In a month no man had come up or down that silent creek. The man held steadily on. He was not much given to thinking, and just then particularly he had nothing to think about save that he would eat lunch at the forks and that at six o'clock he would be in camp with the boys. There was nobody to talk to; and, had there been, speech would have been impossible because of the ice-muzzle on his mouth. So he continued monotonously to chew tobacco and to increase the length of his amber beard.

Once in a while the thought reiterated itself that it was very cold and that he had never experienced such cold. As he walked along he rubbed his cheek-bones and nose with the back of his mittened hand. He did this automatically, now and again changing hands. But rub as he would, the instant he stopped his cheek-bones went numb, and the following instant the end of his nose went numb. He was sure to frost his cheeks; he knew that, and experienced a pang of regret that he had not devised a nose-strap of the sort Bud wore in cold snaps. Such a strap passed across the cheeks, as well, and saved them. But it didn't matter much, after all. What were frosted cheeks? A bit painful, that was all; they were never serious.

Empty as the man's mind was of thoughts, he was keenly observant, and he noticed the changes in the creek, the curves and bends and timber-jams, and always he sharply noted where he placed his feet. Once, coming around a bend, he shied abruptly, like a startled horse, curved away from the place where he had been walking, and retreated several paces back along the trail. The creek he knew was frozen clear to the bottom,—no creek could contain water in that arctic winter,—but he knew also that there were springs that bubbled out from the hillsides and ran along under the snow and on top the ice of the creek. He knew that the coldest snaps never froze these springs, and he knew likewise their danger. They were traps. They hid pools of water under the snow that might be three inches deep, or three feet. Sometimes a skin of ice half an inch thick covered them, and in turn was covered by the snow. Sometimes there were alternate layers of water and ice-skin, so that when one broke through he kept on breaking through for a while, sometimes wetting himself to the waist.

That was why he had shied in such panic. He had felt the give under his feet and heard the crackle of a snow-hidden ice-skin. And to get his feet wet in such a temperature meant trouble and danger. At the very least it meant delay, for he would be forced to stop and build a fire, and under its protection to bare his feet while he dried his socks, and moccasins. He stood and studied the creek-bed and its banks, and decided that the flow of water came from the right. He reflected awhile, rubbing his nose and cheeks, then skirted to the left, stepping gingerly and testing the footing for each step. Once clear of the danger, he took a fresh chew of tobacco and swung along at his four-mile gait.

In the course of the next two hours he came upon several similar traps. Usually the snow above the hidden pools had a sunken, candied appearance that advertised the danger. Once again, however, he had a close call; and once, suspecting danger, he compelled the dog to go on in front. The dog did not want to go. It hung back until the man shoved it forward, and then it went quickly across the white, unbroken surface. Suddenly it broke through, floundered to one side, and got away to firmer footing. It had wet its forefeet and legs, and almost immediately the water that clung to it turned to ice. It made quick efforts to lick the ice off its legs, then dropped down in the snow and began to bite out the ice that had formed between the toes. This was a matter of instinct. To permit the ice to remain would mean sore feet. It did not know this. It merely obeyed the mysterious prompting that arose from the deep crypts of its being. But the man knew, having achieved a judgment on the subject, and he removed the mitten from his right hand and helped tear out the ice-particles. He did not expose his fingers more than a minute, and was astonished at the swift numbness that smote them. It certainly was cold. He pulled on the mitten hastily, and beat the hand savagely across his chest.

At twelve o'clock the day was at its brightest. Yet the sun was too far south on its winter journey to clear the horizon. The bulge of the earth intervened between it and Henderson Creek, where the man walked under a clear sky at noon and cast no shadow. At half-past twelve, to the minute, he arrived at the forks of the creek. He was pleased at the speed he had made. If he kept it up, he would certainly be with the boys by six. He unbuttoned his jacket and shirt and drew forth his lunch. The action consumed no more than a quarter of a minute, yet in that brief moment the numbness laid hold of the exposed fingers. He did not put the mitten on, but, instead, struck the fingers a dozen sharp smashes against his leg. Then he sat down on a snow-covered log to eat. The sting that followed upon the striking of his fingers against his leg ceased so quickly that he was startled. He had had no chance to take a bite of biscuit. He struck the fingers repeatedly and returned them to the mitten, baring the other hand for the purpose of eating. He tried to take a mouthful, but the ice-muzzle prevented. He had forgotten to build a fire and thaw out. He chuckled at his foolishness, and as he chuckled he noted the numbness creeping into the exposed fingers. Also, he noted that the stinging which had first come to his toes when he sat down was already passing away. He wondered whether the toes were warm or numb. He moved them inside the moccasins and decided that they were numb.

He pulled the mitten on hurriedly and stood up. He was a bit frightened. He stamped up and down until the stinging returned into the feet. It certainly was cold, was his thought. That man from Sulphur Creek had spoken the truth when telling how cold it sometimes got in the country. And he had laughed at him at the time! That showed one must not be too sure of things. There was no mistake about it, it *was* cold. He strode up and down, stamping his feet and threshing his arms, until reassured by the returning warmth. Then he got out matches and proceeded to make a fire. From the undergrowth, where high water of the previous spring had lodged a supply of seasoned twigs, he got his fire-wood. Working carefully from a small beginning, he soon had a roaring fire, over which he thawed the ice from his face and in the protection of which he ate his biscuits. For the moment the cold of space was outwitted. The dog took satisfaction in the fire, stretching out close enough for warmth and far enough away to escape being singed.

When the man had finished, he filled his pipe and took his comfortable time over a smoke. Then he pulled on his mittens, settled the earflaps of his cap firmly about his ears, and took the creek trail up the left fork. The dog was disappointed and yearned back toward the fire. This man did not know cold. Possibly all the generations of his ancestry had been ignorant of cold, of real cold one hundred and seven degrees below freezing-point. But the dog knew; all its ancestry knew, and it had inherited the knowledge. And it knew that it was not good to walk abroad in such fearful cold. It was the time to lie snug in a hole in the snow and wait for a curtain of cloud to be drawn across the face of outer space whence this cold came. On the other hand, there was no keen intimacy between the dog and the man. The one was the toil-slave of the other, and the only caresses it had ever received were the caresses of the whip-lash and of harsh and menacing throat-sounds that threatened the whip-lash. So the dog made no effort to communicate its apprehension to the man. It was not concerned in the welfare of the man; it was for its own sake that it yearned back toward the fire. But the man whistled, and spoke to it with the sound of whip-lashes, and the dog swung in at the man's heels and followed after.

The man took a chew of tobacco and proceeded to start a new amber beard. Also, his moist breath quickly powdered with white his mustache, eyebrows, and lashes. There did not seem to be so many springs on the left fork of the Henderson, and for half an hour the man saw no signs of any. And then it happened. At a place where there were no signs, where the soft, unbroken snow seemed to advertise solidity beneath, the man broke through. It was not deep. He wet himself halfway to the knees before he floundered out to the firm crust.

He was angry, and cursed his luck aloud. He had hoped to get into camp with the boys at six o'clock, and this would delay him an hour, for he would have to build a fire and dry out his foot-gear. This was imperative at that low temperature—he knew that much; and he turned aside to the bank, which he climbed. On top, tangled in the underbrush about the trunks of several small spruce trees, was a high-water deposit of dry fire-wood—sticks and twigs, principally, but also larger portions of seasoned branches and fine, dry, last-year's grasses. He threw down several large pieces on top of the snow. This served for a foundation and prevented the young flame from drowning itself in the snow it otherwise would melt. The flame he got by touching a match to a small shred of birch-bark that he took from his pocket. This burned even more readily than paper. Placing it on the foundation, he fed the young flame with wisps of dry grass and with the tiniest dry twigs.

He worked slowly and carefully, keenly aware of his danger. Gradually, as the flame grew stronger, he increased the size of the twigs with which he fed it. He squatted in the snow, pulling the twigs out from their entanglement in the brush and feeding directly to the flame. He knew there must be no failure. When it is seventy-five below zero, a man must not fail in his first attempt to build a fire—that is, if his feet are wet. If his feet are dry, and he fails, he can run along the trail for half a mile and restore his circulation. But the circulation of wet and freezing feet cannot be restored by running when it is seventy-five below. No matter how fast he runs, the wet feet will freeze the harder.

All this the man knew. The old-timer on Sulphur Creek had told him about it the previous fall, and now he was appreciating the advice. Already all sensation had gone out of his feet. To build the fire he had been forced to remove his mittens, and the fingers had quickly gone numb. His pace of four miles an hour had kept his heart pumping blood to the surface of his body and to all the extremities. But the instant he stopped, the action of the pump eased down. The cold of space smote the unprotected tip of the planet, and he, being on that unprotected tip, received the full force of the blow. The blood of his body recoiled before it. The blood was alive, like the dog, and like the dog it wanted to hide away and cover itself up from the fearful cold. So long as he walked four miles an hour, he pumped that blood, willy-nilly, to the surface; but now it ebbed away and sank down into the recesses of his body. The extremities were the first to its absence. His wet feet froze the faster, and his exposed fingers numbed the faster, though they had not yet begun to freeze. Nose and cheeks were already freezing, while the skin of all his body chilled as it lost its blood.

But he was safe. Toes and nose and cheeks would be only touched by the frost, for the fire was beginning to burn with strength. He was feeding it with twigs the size of his finger. In another minute he would be able to feed it with branches the size of his wrist, and then he could remove his wet foot-gear, and, while it dried, he could keep his naked feet warm by the fire, rubbing them at first, of course, with snow. The fire was a success. He was safe. He remembered the advice of the old-timer on Sulphur Creek, and smiled. The old-timer had been very serious in laying down the law that no man must travel alone in the Klondike after fifty below. Well, here he was; he had had the accident; he was alone; and he had saved himself. Those old-timers were rather womanish, some of them, he thought. All a man had to do was to keep his head, and he was all right. Any man who was a man could travel alone. But it was surprising, the rapidity with which his cheeks and nose were freezing. And he had not thought his fingers could go lifeless in so short a time. Lifeless they were, for he could scarcely make them move together to grip a twig, and they seemed remote from his body and from him. When he touched a twig, he had to look and see whether or not he had hold of it. The wires were pretty well down between him and his finger-ends.

All of which counted for little. There was a fire, snapping and crackling and promising life with every dancing flame. He started to untie his moccasins. They were coated with ice; the thick German socks were like sheaths of iron halfway to the knees; and the moccasin strings were like rods of steel all twisted and knotted as by some conflagration. For a moment he tugged with his numb fingers, then, realizing the folly of it, he drew his sheath-knife.

But before he could cut the strings, it happened. It was his own fault or, rather, his mistake. He should not have built the fire under the spruce tree. He should have built it in the open. But it had been easier to pull the twigs from the brush and drop them directly on the fire. Now the tree under which he had done this carried a weight of snow on its boughs. No wind had blown for weeks, and each bough was fully freighted. Each time he had pulled a twig he had communicated a slight agitation to the tree —an imperceptible agitation, so far as he was concerned, but an agitation sufficient to bring about the disaster. High up in the tree one bough capsized its load of snow. This fell on the boughs beneath, capsizing them. This process continued, spreading out and involving the whole tree. It grew like an avalanche, and it descended without warning upon the man and the fire, and the fire was blotted out! Where it had burned was a mantle of fresh and disordered snow.

The man was shocked. It was as though he had just heard his own sentence of death. For a moment he sat and stared at the spot where the fire had been. Then he grew very calm. Perhaps the old-timer on Sulphur Creek was right. If he had only had a trail-mate he would have been in no danger now. The trail-mate could have built the fire. Well, it was up to him to build the fire over again, and this second time there must be no failure. Even if he succeeded, he would most likely lose some toes. His feet must be badly frozen by now, and there would be some time before the second fire was ready.

Such were his thoughts, but he did not sit and think them. He was busy all the time they were passing through his mind. He made a new foundation for a fire, this time in the open, where no treacherous tree could blot it out. Next, he gathered dry grasses and tiny twigs from the high-water flotsam. He could not bring his fingers together to pull them out, but he was able to gather them by the handful. In this way he got many rotten twigs and bits of green moss that were undesirable, but it was the best he could do. He worked methodically, even collecting an armful of the larger branches to be used later when the fire gathered strength. And all the while the dog sat and watched him, a certain yearning wistfulness in its eyes,

for it looked upon him as the fire-provider, and the fire
was slow in coming.

When all was ready, the man reached in his pocket for
a second piece of birch-bark. He knew the bark was
there, and, though he could not feel it with his fingers, he
could hear its crisp rustling as he fumbled for it. Try as
he would, he could not clutch hold of it. And all the time,
in his consciousness, was the knowledge that each instant
his feet were freezing. This thought tended to put him in
a panic, but he fought against it and kept calm. He pulled
on his mittens with his teeth, and threshed his arms back
and forth, beating his hands with all his might against his
sides. He did this sitting down, and he stood up to do it;
and all the while the dog sat in the snow, its wolf-brush
of a tail curled around warmly over its forefeet, its sharp
wolf-ears pricked forward intently as it watched the man.
And the man, as he beat and threshed with his arms and
hands, felt a great surge of envy as he regarded the creature that was warm and secure in its natural covering.

After a time he was aware of the first far-away signals
of sensation in his beaten fingers. The faint tingling grew
stronger till it evolved into a stinging ache that was excru-
ciating, but which the man hailed with satisfaction. He
stripped the mitten from his right hand and fetched forth
the birch-bark. The exposed fingers were quickly going
numb again. Next he brought out his bunch of sulphur
matches. But the tremendous cold had already driven the
life out of his fingers. In his effort to separate one match
from the others, the whole bunch fell in the snow. He
tried to pick it out of the snow, but failed. The dead fingers could neither touch nor clutch. He was very careful.
He drove the thought of his freezing feet, and nose, and
cheeks, out of his mind, devoting his whole soul to the
matches. He watched, using the sense of vision in place of
that of touch, and when he saw his fingers on each side of
the bunch, he closed them—that is, he willed to close
them, for the wires were down, and the fingers did not
obey. He pulled the mitten on the right hand, and beat it
fiercely against his knee. Then, with both mittened hands,

he scooped the bunch of matches, along with much snow, into his lap. Yet he was no better off.

After some manipulation he managed to get the bunch between the heels of his mittened hands. In this fashion he carried it to his mouth. The ice crackled and snapped when by a violent effort he opened his mouth. He drew the lower jaw in, curled the upper lip out of the way, and scraped the bunch with his upper teeth in order to separate a match. He succeeded in getting one, which he dropped on his lap. He was no better off. He could not pick it up. Then he devised a way. He picked it up in his teeth and scratched it on his leg. Twenty times he scratched before he succeeded in lighting it. As it flamed he held it with his teeth to the birch-bark. But the burning brimstone went up his nostrils and into his lungs, causing him to cough spasmodically. The match fell into the snow and went out.

The old-timer on Sulphur Creek was right, he thought in the moment of controlled despair that ensued: after fifty below, a man should travel with a partner. He beat his hands, but failed in exciting any sensation. Suddenly he bared both hands, removing the mittens with his teeth. He caught the whole bunch between the heels of his hands. His arm-muscles not being frozen enabled him to press the hand-heels tightly against the matches. Then he scratched the bunch along his leg. It flared into flame, seventy sulphur matches at once! There was no wind to blow them out. He kept his head to one side to escape the strangling fumes, and held the blazing bunch to the birch-bark. As he so held it, he became aware of sensation in his hand. His flesh was burning. He could smell it. Deep down below the surface he could feel it. The sensation developed into pain that grew acute. And still he endured it, holding the flame of the matches clumsily to the bark that would not light readily because his own burning hands were in the way, absorbing most of the flame.

At last, when he could endure no more, he jerked his hands apart. The blazing matches fell sizzling into the snow, but the birch-bark was alight. He began laying dry grasses and the tiniest twigs on the flame. He could not pick and choose, for he had to lift the fuel between the heels of his hands. Small pieces of rotten wood and green moss clung to the twigs, and he bit them off as well as he could with his teeth. He cherished the flame carefully and awkwardly. It meant life, and it must not perish. The withdrawal of blood from the surface of his body now made him begin to shiver, and he grew more awkward. A large piece of green moss fell squarely on the little fire. He tried to poke it out with his fingers, but his shivering frame made him poke too far, and he disrupted the nucleus of the little fire, the burning grasses and tiny twigs separating and scattering. He tried to poke them together again, but in spite of the tenseness of the effort, his shivering got away with him, and the twigs were hopelessly scattered. Each twig gushed a puff of smoke and went out. The fire-provider had failed. As he looked apathetically about him, his eyes chanced on the dog, sitting across the ruins of the fire from him, in the snow, making restless, hunching movements, slightly lifting one forefoot and then the other, shifting its weight back and forth on them with wistful eagerness.

The sight of the dog put a wild idea into his head. He remembered the tale of the man, caught in a blizzard, who killed a steer and crawled inside the carcass, and so was saved. He would kill the dog and bury his hands in the warm body until the numbness went out of them. Then he could build another fire. He spoke to the dog, calling it to him; but in his voice was a strange note of fear that frightened the animal, who had never known the man to speak in such way before. Something was the matter, and its suspicious nature sensed danger—it knew not what danger, but somewhere, somehow, in its brain arose an apprehension of the man. It flattened its ears down at the sound of the man's voice, and its restless, hunching movements and liftings and shiftings of its forefeet became more pronounced; but it would not come to the man. He got on his hands and knees and crawled toward the dog. This unusual posture again excited suspicion, and the animal sidled mincingly away.

The man sat up in the snow for a moment and struggled for calmness. Then he pulled on his mittens, by means of his teeth, and got upon his feet. He glanced down at first in order to assure himself that he was really standing up, for the absence of sensation in his feet left him unrelated to the earth. His erect position in itself started to drive the webs of suspicion from the dog's mind; and when he spoke peremptorily, with the sound of whip-lashes in his voice, the dog rendered its customary allegiance and came to him. As it came within reaching distance, the man lost his control. His arms flashed out to the dog, and he experienced genuine surprise when he discovered that his hands could not clutch, that there was neither bend nor feeling in the fingers. He had forgotten for the moment that they were frozen and that they were freezing more and more. All this happened quickly, and before the animal could get away, he encircled its body with his arms. He sat down in the snow, and in this fashion held the dog, while it snarled and whined and struggled.

But it was all he could do, hold its body encircled in his arms and sit there. He realized that he could not kill the dog. There was no way to do it. With his helpless hands he could neither draw nor hold his sheath-knife nor throttle the animal. He released it, and it plunged wildly away, with tail between its legs, and still snarling. It halted forty feet away and surveyed him curiously, with ears sharply pricked forward. The man looked down at his hands in order to locate them, and found them hanging on the ends of his arms. It struck him as curious that one should have to use his eyes in order to find out where his hands were. He began threshing his arms back and forth, beating the mittened hands against his sides. He did this for five minutes, violently, and his heart pumped enough blood up to the surface to put a stop to his shivering. But no sensation was aroused in the hands. He had an impression that they hung like weights on the ends of his arms, but when he tried to run the impression down, he could not find it.

A certain fear of death, dull and oppressive, came to him. This fear quickly became poignant as he realized

that it was no longer a mere matter of freezing his fingers
and toes, or of losing his hands and feet, but that it was a
matter of life and death with the chances against him.
This threw him into a panic, and he turned and ran up
the creek-bed along the old, dim trail. The dog joined in
behind and kept up with him. He ran blindly, without intention, in fear such as he had never known in his life.
Slowly, as he ploughed and floundered through the snow,
he began to see things again,—the banks of the creek, the
old timber-jams, the leafless aspens, and the sky. The
running made him feel better. He did not shiver. Maybe,
if he ran on, his feet would thaw out; and, anyway, if he
ran far enough, he would reach camp and the boys.
Without doubt he would lose some fingers and toes and
some of his face; but the boys would take care of him,
and save the rest of him when he got there. And at the
same time there was another thought in his mind that said
he would never get to the camp and the boys; that it was
too many miles away, that the freezing had too great a
start on him, and that he would soon be stiff and dead.
This thought he kept in the background and refused to
consider. Sometimes it pushed itself forward and demand-
ed to be heard, but he thrust it back and strove to think
of other things.

It struck him as curious that he could run at all on feet
so frozen that he could not feel them when they struck
the earth and took the weight of his body. He seemed to
himself to skim along above the surface, and to have no
connection with the earth. Somewhere he had once seen a
winged Mercury, and he wondered if Mercury felt as he
felt when skimming over the earth.

His theory of running until he reached camp and the
boys had one flaw in it: he lacked the endurance. Several
times he stumbled, and finally he tottered, crumpled up,
and fell. When he tried to rise, he failed. He must sit and
rest, he decided, and next time he would merely walk and
keep on going. As he sat and regained his breath, he
noted that he was feeling quite warm and comfortable.
He was not shivering, and it even seemed that a warm
glow had come to his chest and trunk. And yet, when he

touched his nose or cheeks, there was no sensation. Running would not thaw them out. Nor would it thaw out his hands and feet. Then the thought came to him that the frozen portions of his body must be extending. He tried to keep this thought down, to forget it, to think of something else; he was aware of the panicky feeling that it caused, and he was afraid of the panic. But the thought asserted itself, and persisted, until it produced a vision of his body totally frozen. This was too much, and he made another wild run along the trail. Once he slowed down to a walk, but the thought of the freezing extending itself made him run again.

And all the time the dog ran with him, at his heels. When he fell down a second time, it curled its tail over its forefeet and sat in front of him, facing him, curiously eager and intent. The warmth and security of the animal angered him, and he cursed it till it flattened down its ears appeasingly. This time the shivering came more quickly upon the man. He was losing in his battle with the frost. It was creeping into his body from all sides. The thought of it drove him on, but he ran no more than a hundred feet, when he staggered and pitched headlong. It was his last panic. When he had recovered his breath and control, he sat up and entertained in his mind the conception of meeting death with dignity. However, the conception did not come to him in such terms. His idea of it was that he had been making a fool of himself, running around like a chicken with its head cut off—such was the simile that occurred to him. Well, he was bound to freeze anyway, and he might as well take it decently. With this new-found peace of mind came the first glimmerings of drowsiness. A good idea, he thought, to sleep off to death. It was like taking an anæsthetic. Freezing was not so bad as people thought. There were lots worse ways to die.

He pictured the boys finding his body next day. Suddenly he found himself with them, coming along the trail and looking for himself. And, still with them, he came around a turn in the trail and found himself lying in the snow. He did not belong with himself any more, for even then he was out of himself, standing with the boys and looking at himself in the snow. It certainly was cold, was his thought. When he got back to the States he could tell the folks what real cold was. He drifted on from this to a vision of the old-timer on Sulpher Creek. He could see him quite clearly, warm and comfortable, and smoking a pipe.

"You were right, old hoss; you were right," the man mumbled to the old-timer of Sulphur Creek.

Then the man drowsed off into what seemed to him the most comfortable and satisfying sleep he had ever known. The dog sat facing him and waiting. The brief day drew to a close in a long, slow twilight. There were no signs of a fire to be made, and besides, never in the dog's experience had it known a man to sit like that in the snow and make no fire. As the twilight drew on, its eager yearning for the fire mastered it, and with a great lifting and shifting of forefeet, it whined softly, then flattened its ears down in anticipation of being chidden by the man. But the man remained silent. Later, the dog whined loudly. And still later it crept close to the man and caught the scent of death. This made the animal bristle and back away. A little longer it delayed, howling under the stars that leaped and danced and shone brightly in the cold sky. Then it turned and trotted up the trail in the direction of the camp it knew, where were the other food-providers and fire-providers.

LOCOMOTIVE 38, THE OJIBWAY

by William Saroyan

ONE DAY a man came to town on a donkey and began loafing around in the public library where I used to spend most of my time in those days. He was a tall young Indian of the Ojibway tribe. He told me his name was Locomotive 38. Everybody in town believed he had escaped from an asylum.

Six days after he arrived in town his animal was struck by the Tulare Street trolley and seriously injured. The following day the animal passed away, most likely of internal injuries, on the corner of Mariposa and Fulton streets. The animal sank to the pavement, fell on the Indian's leg, groaned and died. When the Indian got his leg free he got up and limped into the drug store on the corner and made a long distance telephone call. He telephoned his brother in Oklahoma. The call cost him a lot of money, which he dropped into the slot as requested by the operator as if he were in the habit of making such calls every day.

I was in the drug store at the time, eating a Royal Banana Special, with crushed walnuts.

When he came out of the telephone booth he saw me sitting at the soda fountain eating this fancy dish.

Hello, Willie, he said.

He knew my name wasn't Willie—he just liked to call me that.

115

He limped to the front of the store where the gum was, and bought three packages of Juicy Fruit. Then he limped back to me and said, What's that you're eating, Willie? It looks good.

This is what they call a Royal Banana Special, I said.

The Indian got up on the stool next to me.

Give me the same, he said to the soda fountain girl.

That's too bad about your animal, I said.

There's no place for an animal in this world, he said. What kind of an automobile should I buy?

Are you going to buy an automobile? I said.

I've been thinking about it for several minutes now, he said.

I didn't think you had any money, I said. I thought you were poor.

That's the impression people get, he said. Another impression they get is that I'm crazy.

I didn't get the impression that you were crazy, I said, but I didn't get the impression that you were rich, either.

Well, I am, the Indian said.

I wish I was rich, I said.

What for? he said.

Well, I said, I've been wanting to go fishing at Mendota for three years in a row now. I need some equipment and some kind of an automobile to get out there in.

Can you drive an automobile? the Indian said.

I can drive anything, I said.

Have you ever driven an automobile? he said.

Not yet, I said. So far I haven't had any automobile to drive, and it's against my family religion to steal an automobile.

Do you mean to tell me you believe you could get into an automobile and start driving? he said.

That's right, I said.

Remember what I was telling you on the steps of the public library the other evening? he said.

You mean about the machine age? I said.

Yes, he said.

I remember, I said.

All right, he said. Indians are born with an instinct for riding, rowing, hunting, fishing, and swimming. Americans are born with an instinct for fooling around with machines.

I am no American, I said.

I know, the Indian said. You're an Armenian. I remember. I asked you and you told me. You're an Armenian born in America. You're fourteen years old and already you know you'll be able to drive an automobile the minute you get into one. You're a typical American, although your complexion, like my own, is dark.

Driving a car is no trick, I said. There's nothing to it. It's easier than riding a donkey.

All right, the Indian said. Just as you say. If I go up the street and buy an automobile, will you drive for me?

Of course, I said.

How much in wages would you want? he said.

You mean you want to give me wages for driving an automobile? I said.

Of course, the Ojibway said.

Well, I said, that's very nice of you, but I don't want any money for driving an automobile.

Some of the journeys may be long ones, he said.

The longer the better, I said.

Are you restless? he said.

I was born in this little old town, I said.

Don't you like it? he said.

I like mountains and streams and mountain lakes, I said.

Have you ever been in the mountains? he said.

Not yet, I said, but I'm going to reach them some day.

I see, he said. What kind of an automobile do you think I ought to buy?

How about a Ford roadster? I said.

Is that the best automobile? he said.

Do you want the *best?* I said.

Shouldn't I have the best? he said.

I don't know, I said. The best costs a lot of money.

What is the best? he said.

Well, I said, some people think the Cadillac is the best.

Others like the Packard. They're both pretty good. I wouldn't know which is best. The Packard is beautiful to see going down the highway, but so is the Cadillac. I've watched a lot of them fine cars going down the highway.

How much is a Packard? he said.

Around three thousand dollars, I said. Maybe a little more.

Can we get one right away? he said.

I got down off the stool. He sounded crazy, but I knew he wasn't.

Listen, Mr. Locomotive, I said, do you really want to buy a Packard right away?

You know my animal passed away a few minutes ago, he said.

I saw it happen, I said. They'll probably be arresting you any minute now for leaving the animal in the street.

They won't arrest me, he said.

They will if there's a law against leaving a dead donkey in the street, I said.

No, they won't, he said.

Why not? I said.

Well, he said, they won't after I show them a few papers I carry around with me all the time. The people of this country have a lot of respect for money, and I've got a lot of money.

I guess he is crazy after all, I thought.

Where'd you get all this money? I said.

I own some land in Oklahoma, he said. About fifty thousand acres.

Is it worth money? I said.

No, he said. All but about twenty acres of it is worthless. I've got some oil wells on them twenty acres. My brother and I.

How did you Ojibways ever get down to Oklahoma? I said. I always thought the Ojibways lived up north, up around the Great lakes.

That's right, the Indian said. We used to live up around the Great Lakes, but my grandfather was a pioneer. He moved west when everybody else did.

Oh, I said. Well, I guess they won't bother you about the dead donkey at that.

They won't bother me about anything, he said. It won't be because I've got money. It'll be because they think I'm crazy. Nobody in this town but you knows I've got money. Do you know where we can get one of them automobiles right away?

The Packard agency is up on Broadway, two blocks beyond the public library, I said.

All right, he said. If you're sure you won't mind driving for me, let's go get one of them. Something bright in color, he said. Red, if they've got red. Where would you like to drive to first?

Would you care to go fishing at Mendota? I said.

I'll take the ride, he said. I'll watch you fish. Where can we get some equipment for you?

Right around the corner at Homan's, I said.

We went around the corner to Homan's and the Indian bought twenty-seven dollars' worth of fishing equipment for me. Then we went up to the Packard agency on Broadway. They didn't have a red Packard, but there was a beautiful green one. It was light green, the color of new grass. This was back there in 1922. The car was a beautiful sports touring model.

Do you think you could drive this great big car? the Indian said.

I *know* I can drive it, I said.

The police found us in the Packard agency and wanted to arrest the Indian for leaving the dead donkey in the street. He showed them the papers he had told me about and the police apologized and went away. They said they'd removed the animal and were sorry they'd troubled him about it.

It's no trouble at all, he said

He turned to the manager of the Packard agency, Jim Lewis, who used to run for Mayor every time election time came around.

I'll take this car, he said.

I'll draw up the papers immediately, Jim said.

What papers? the Indian said. I'm going to pay for it now.

You mean you want to pay three thousand two hundred seventeen dollars and sixty-five cents *cash?* Jim said.

Yes, the Indian said. It's ready to drive, isn't it?

Of course, Jim said. I'll have the boys go over it with a cloth to take off any dust on it. I'll have them check the motor too, and fill the gasoline tank. It won't take more than ten minutes. If you'll step into the office I'll close the transaction immediately.

Jim and the Indian stepped into Jim's office.

About three minutes later Jim came over to me, a man shaken to the roots.

Aram, he said, who is this guy? I thought he was a nut. I had Johnny telephone the Pacific-Southwest and they said his bank account is being transferred from somewhere in Oklahoma. They said his account is something over a million dollars. I thought he was a nut. Do you know him?

He told me his name is Locomotive 38, I said. That's no name.

That's a translation of his Indian name, Jim said. We've got his full name on the contract. Do you know him?

I've talked to him every day since he came to town on that donkey that died this morning, I said, but I never thought he had any money.

He says you're going to drive for him, Jim said. Are you sure you're the man to drive a great big car like this, son?

Wait a minute now, Mr. Lewis, I said. Don't try to push me out of this chance of a lifetime. I can drive this Packard as well as anybody else in town.

I'm not trying to push you out of anything, Jim said. I just don't want you to drive out of here and run over six or seven innocent people and maybe smash the car. Get into the car and I'll give you a few pointers. Do you know anything about the gear shift?

I don't know anything about anything yet, I said, but I'll soon find out.

All right, Jim said. Just let me help you.

I got into the car and sat down behind the wheel. Jim got in beside me.

From now on, son, he said, I want you to regard me as a friend who will give you the shirt off his back. I want to thank you for bringing me this fine Indian gentleman.

He told me he wanted the best car on the market, I said. You know I've always been crazy about driving a Packard. Now how do I do it?

Well, Jim said, let's see.

He looked down at my feet.

My God, son, he said, your feet don't reach the pedals.

Never mind that, I said. You just explain the gear shift.

Jim explained everything while the boys wiped the dust off the car and went over the motor and filled the gasoline tank. When the Indian came out and got into the car, in the back where I insisted he should sit, I had the motor going.

He says he knows how to drive, the Indian said to Jim Lewis. By instinct, he said. I believe him, too.

You needn't worry about Aram here, Jim said. He can drive all right. Clear the way there, boys, he shouted. Let him have all the room necessary.

I turned the big car around slowly, shifted, and shot out of the agency at about fifty miles an hour, with Jim Lewis running after the car and shouting, Take it easy, son. Don't open up until you get out on the highway. The speed limit in town is twenty-five miles an hour.

The Indian wasn't at all excited, even though I was throwing him around a good deal.

I wasn't doing it on purpose, though. It was simply that I wasn't very familiar with the manner in which the automobile worked.

You're an excellent driver, Willie, he said. It's like I said. You're an American and you were born with an instinct for mechanical contraptions like this.

We'll be in Mendota in an hour, I said. You'll see some great fishing out there.

How far is Mendota? the Indian said.

About ninety miles, I said.

Ninety miles is too far to go in an hour, the Indian said. Take two hours. We're passing a lot of interesting scenery I'd like to look at a little more closely.

All right, I said, but I sure am anxious to get out there and fish.

Well, all right then, the Indian said. Go as fast as you like this time, but some time I'll expect you to drive a little more slowly, so I can see some of the scenery. I'm missing everything. I don't even get a chance to read the signs.

I'll travel slowly *now* if you want me to, I said.

No, he insisted. Let her go. Let her go as fast as she'll go.

Well, we got out to Mendota in an hour and seventeen minutes. I would have made better time except for the long stretch of dirt road.

I drove the car right up to the river bank. The Indian asked if I knew how to get the top down, so he could sit in the open and watch me fish. I didn't know how to get the top down, but I got it down. It took me twenty minutes to do it.

I fished for about three hours, fell into the river twice, and finally landed a small one.

You don't know the first thing about fishing, the Indian said.

What am I doing wrong? I said.

Everything, he said. Have you ever fished before?

No, I said.

I didn't think so, he said.

What am I doing wrong? I said.

Well, he said, nothing in particular, only you're fishing at about the same rate of speed that you drive an automobile.

Is that wrong? I said.

It's not exactly wrong, he said, except that it'll keep you from getting anything to speak of, and you'll go on falling into the river.

I'm not falling, I said. They're pulling me in. They've got an awful pull. This grass is mighty slippery, too. There ain't nothing around here to grab hold of.

I reeled in one more little one and then I asked if he'd like to go home. He said he would if I wanted to, too, so I put away the fishing equipment and the two fish and got in the car and started driving back to town.

I drove that big Packard for this Ojibway Indian, Locomotive 38, as long as he stayed in town, which was all summer. He stayed at the hotel all the time. I tried to get him to learn to drive, but he said it was out of the question. I drove that Packard all over the San Joaquín Valley that summer, with the Indian in the back, chewing eight or nine sticks of gum. He told me to drive anywhere I cared to go, so it was either to some place where I could fish, or some place where I could hunt. He claimed I didn't know anything about fishing or hunting, but he was glad to see me trying. As long as I knew him he never laughed, except once. That was the time I shot at a jack-rabbit with a 12-gauge shotgun that had a terrible kick, and killed a crow. He tried to tell me all the time that that was my average. To shoot at a jack-rabbit and kill a crow. You're an American, he said. Look at the way you took to this big automobile.

One day in November that year his brother came to town from Oklahoma, and the next day when I went down to the hotel to get him, they told me he'd gone back to Oklahoma with his brother.

Where's the Packard? I said.

They took the Packard, the hotel clerk said.

Who drove? I said.

The Indian, the clerk said.

They're both Indians, I said. Which of the brothers drove the car?

The one who lived at this hotel, the clerk said.

Are you sure? I said.

Well, I only saw him get into the car out front and drive away, the clerk said. That's all.

Do you mean to tell me he knew how to shift gears? I said.

It *looked* as if he did, the clerk said. He looked like an expert driver to me.

Thanks, I said.

On the way home I figured he'd just wanted me to *believe* he couldn't drive, so *I* could drive all the time and feel good. He was just a young man who'd come to town on a donkey, bored to death or something, who'd taken advantage of the chance to be entertained by a small town kid who was bored to death, too. That's the only way I could figure it out without accepting the general theory that he was crazy.

HIGH AIR

by Borden Chase

DEEP UNDER THE RIVER BED an iron monster gnawed
at the muck and slime. It breathed. And great lungfuls of
highly compressed air rose in gurgling bubbles through
the swift moving water to burst as foaming froth at the
surface. Crunching, grinding, swallowing, tearing at the
sand and earth with sharp steel jaws, the gargantuan reptile slithered along. Heavy iron plates formed for it an
armor that put to shame the protective covering of prehistoric beasts. Thrusting ever deeper, forward, with irresistible force, it shuddered the earth with its efforts. The sandhogs were building a river tunnel.

Strange men these sandhogs. Strange men working at a
strange trade. Above them the river moved with quiet
dignity to the sea. Scurrying tugboats warped the graceful
ocean liners to docks. Swift moving ferryboats panted im-
patient blasts at sluggish barges. Graceful bridges
stretched their delicate arcs over the glistening stream,
linking the boroughs of a mighty city. A pleasant world.
A world of sunshine and gentle breezes, of crisp cold air
that smiled with a hint of spring.

Ninety feet below the shimmering surface of the river,
the hollow-eyed sandhogs inhabited a different world. A
world where a gale continually raged. A man-made tempest, scorching blasts of highly compressed air fed to the
toilers in the tunnel. Compressed air—vile stuff that often
twisted their limbs with indescribable agonies, tortured
their lungs or sent them reeling, staggering into eternity.
Air—sucked into the whirling compressors, pounded by

the thrusting pistons until it roared through the long black pipes that led to the tunnel. Air—that sapped the very life from the sandhogs' veins. Devilish stuff, fiendish stuff —but it kept the river out.

In the company restaurant near the tunnel shaft, the stamp of heavy boots rose above the roar of many voices. Sandhogs sat at the tables or stood against the long counter at the rear of the room. Tobacco smoke hung heavy above their heads. No cleansing drafts disturbed the sluggish cloud. The windows were tightly closed and the heat danced in waves from the steam pipes along the base of the walls. The reek of wet clothes and the sweet odor of alcohol mingled with the stench of grease burning on an open range behind the counter.

The men wore heavy sheepskin coats, for the pores of their skin must be kept open to allow the compressed air to seep out of their bodies. Long woolen underwear, khaki shirts, and grimy trousers thrust into high boots completed the outfit. Each table held its quota of card players and voices were loud as the bets ran high. Flasks of whiskey went round. Sudden argument flared into fight. There was that tension in the room which prevails whenever men are jealous of the flying minutes.

The tunnel was deep and forty pounds of air were holding back the river. The working time was short—one hour shifts and between them five hours in which to rest. But the sandhog's idea of rest was to live hard—live fast —drag each full measure of life from the hours of freedom. The talk was of tunnels—tunnels that had been built and rivers that had been conquered. Men shouted, laughed, and boasted. The Klondike in its wildest days never knew a gambling hell to surpass the restaurant of the sandhogs. Only the women were missing—the tunnel is a man's game.

In a far corner of the room two men faced each other across a rough wooden table. Joe Redman, veteran of many tunnels, clenched his pipe tightly between his teeth as he studied his son.

"So you had to come back, eh, kid?" he grunted.

"Couldn't keep away when they put a few pounds of air on the job. Why?"

"I don't know." Steve grinned as he shuffled his empty coffee cup about the table. His eyes, when he lifted them to look at his father, were the same deep blue as the older man's. His shoulders were just as broad, his flanks as narrow. Save for a few streaks of gray in the father's hair and an indefinite touch that comes with years, they might have been brothers.

"Weren't you satisfied at school?"

"Oh, that had nothing to do with it. I liked it well enough—wanted to become an engineer—but it's the tunnel. You know, dad, it gets you."

"Yes, I know. It's something I've been worrying about ever since you worked your first job. Give a man a taste of high air and that ends it. If he's born to be a sandhog, the stuff gets into his blood and there's no cure for it." He paused. The smoke from his pipe rose in a lazy cloud to join the heavy mass above. "How old were you when you first came to work in the tunnel with me?"

"Fifteen. It was during my summer vacation while I was at high school. You were out on that Detroit River job."

"Mmmm," said Joe, His blue eyes studied the boy. "Just a kid, weren't you? But you wanted to be a sandhog like your old man."

"I was big enough to handle a shovel."

"Yeah, big enough to handle a shovel—that's it. That's when I started—and your grandfather, too. Big enough to handle a shovel in the Redman family means big enough to start eating high air—big enough to get the bends, the chokes, yeah—big enough to get paralyzed and die. But I thought it was going to be different with you."

"Now look here, dad, you're not going through all that stuff again, are you?"

"No, I guess not. It wouldn't do any good. You're here, you have made up your mind to go sandhogging again and that's that. Now there is only one question."

"What?"

"Does your mother know you are here?"

"No." Steve was less the man and more the boy as he spoke. His eyes dropped momentarily and a slight flush rose to his temples. "Wouldn't it be better if we didn't talk about her?"

"Yes, it might be. But I'm afraid we have to. Do you know how long it is since I have seen your mother?"

"Five years, isn't it?"

"That's right, five years. And it is just five years ago that I let you work in a tunnel. Your mother and I had our first quarrel when you came home bragging about being a sandhog. Oh, we'd had little spats now and then but that was the first one that amounted to anything. She told me it was the cruelest thing I had ever done. I laughed. I said you were born to be a tunnel man."

He jammed one calloused finger into the pipe bowl and tamped the tobacco. Slowly he wiped the ash from his finger against his grimy trouser leg. "Things didn't seem to go right for us after that. I came East to work on a job and she stayed in Detroit. I wrote but I only got one answer—she said I'd stolen her son."

The silence between the two men was age-long. Steve slid the empty coffee cup from hand to hand. He drew his finger across the wet table top and studied the mark that it left. Twice he seemed about to speak but did not. His father's pipe made blue clouds above their heads. The noisy confusion of the crowded restaurant swept round them unnoticed. At length Steve lifted his eyes.

"And that is the reason you and mother are. . . ?"

"That's it," said Joe. The words were short, clipped, harsh. "That's why I sent you to college. That's why I wanted you to stay there. But—" and he smiled—"it didn't work, did it, kid? By the way, who gave you the job?"

"Big Tim Martin. He's taking me in with the gang on the next shift."

Joe Redman pushed back his chair. He crossed the room and stood for a moment behind a broad-shouldered giant at one of the tables. Big Tim looked up from his cards and cupped a hand to his ear. A wide grin creased

his features and he nodded in vigorous approval. Joe left
the table and returned to his son.

"That's settled," he grunted.

"You didn't tell him to lay me off?" Anxiety was in
Steve's voice.

"No. What good would that do? You would only go
down with one of the other gangs. I just told him I was
going to work the center pocket for him, that's all."

"In other words," said Steve, "you don't trust me alone
in the heading."

"No-o-o—it's not exactly that, Steve. I guess you'll
make a fairly good miner. But the way you acted to-day
—that's not so good."

"What do you mean?"

"Well, yesterday you got my letter. I told you we were
pretty well under the river. That was a mistake. I
shouldn't have mentioned the tunnel. But I did, and here
you are signed up with a gang the next day. That's snap
judgment, son. That stuff kills men under the river if they
guess wrong."

Resentment flared into Steve's eyes. A swift answer
sprang to his lips. The hair-trigger temper of a Redman
leaped up. But a full-throated bellow from Big Tim interrupted.

"Let's go!"

The cry rang loud above the confusion of the room.
The towering heading boss arose and started toward the
door. The men of his gang dropped their cards or hastily
finished a hand.

"Let's go!"

The sandhogs fastened the heavy coat collars tightly
about their throats. The men streamed through the door
and headed for the shaft.

At the top of the shaft a stout wooden gantry straddled
the width of the street. The gang climbed the long flight
of stairs to the upper deck. In the center of the platform
fast-moving cages brought wet sand from the river bed in
small iron muck-cars. Men wheeled flat-cars carrying
curved iron segments onto the empty cages and they were
lowered swiftly.

Joe Redman and his son crowded with the men of Big Tim's gang onto an empty cage.

"Cut the rope!" The command came from the heading boss and the elevator dropped rapidly down the narrow shaft. A moist cold rose from the sump beneath as the light of day gave place to flaring electric bulbs. The sandhogs huddled closely together for warmth. The wet steel sides of the caisson flashed past as the car fell. There was a slight jar. The men stepped from the cage and walked to the concrete bulkhead blocking the mouth of the tunnel.

The ends of three massive iron cylinders projected from the bulkhead. Bolt studded iron doors were set in the center of each. To the left was the muck-lock through which the sand was carted from the tunnel. Beside it was the man-lock. Above, as close to the roof of the tunnel as it could be squeezed was the emergency lock—the last refuge of the sandhogs in the event of a blow. Should the river break through and flood the heading they were offered one avenue of escape—the emergency lock.

Big Tim stepped to the door of the man-lock. He picked up a bolt and knocked against the iron flange. A deafening roar of escaping air blasted into the shaft. The roar mounted to a shrill scream—then faded to a low wail.

The door groaned with the releasing pressure and swung open. Into the long iron cylinder stepped the gang. Joe stood to one side as Steve ducked his head beneath the low portal. He laid a friendly hand upon the boy's back and followed him into the lock. Crouching, the others crowded in and seated themselves on the wooden benches along the sides. Big Tim put his shoulder to the door. It closed with a muffled boom as the rubber gasket flushed with the diaphragm.

"All set?" He glanced along the two lines of waiting men. "Open it up!"

At the far end of the lock was a recording gauge. Before it sat the lock-tender. He reached to the valve above his head and jerked it open. The air screamed into the lock. The rapid compression generated a stifling heat; it burned with the breath of a blast furnace. The pointer on the gauge rose rapidly—five pounds—ten pounds—fifteen—twenty—

"How's the ears?" yelled Joe above the strident howling of the air.

Steve nodded assurance. He held his nose and forced the air into the upper passages of his head to equalize the pressure. Beside him on the long benches the sandhogs were gaping and blowing. The heat increased. Steadily the finger of the gauge rose. The scream of the air beat against their eardrums. Joe smiled and winked at the boy. Steve grinned. Slowly the blast lessened. It stopped. The inner door of the lock moaned. There was a dull swish as the gasket released and the massive portal swung inward. The gauge showed forty pounds.

As the sandhogs stepped from the lock, the length of the tunnel stretched before them in misty darkness. The lights twinkled dully through the ever-present haze.

"Glad to get back, kid?" asked Joe. They walked slowly down the slight incline toward the heading. Narrow gauge tracks divided the wooden flooring of the tunnel. Steve placed one hand on his father's shoulder to balance himself as he walked one of the rails.

"It's great, dad. There's something about the tunnel— the high air—the—oh, I don't know what it is. I used to think of all this while I was at school. Finally I couldn't stick it any longer. I had to come back."

"You're welcome to it," growled Joe. "I hope I never see the inside of another tunnel. Sometimes I think I won't."

"Go on—don't make me laugh," smiled Steve. "As long as they build these things you'll be down here eating high air."

"Maybe, but I doubt it." Gradually he slowed until they were a few yards behind the gang. "Say, kid, when did you hear from your mother?"

"Last week, I think."

"Does she ever mention me?"

"Sure, lots of times."

"She does?" The veiled eagerness in Joe's voice was lost to his son. "What does she say?"

"Oh, all kinds of things. Wants to know how you are and all that. She asked me if you still get the bends in your arm every week or so?"

"Yeah? Well, when you write her again, tell her—"

But Joe was left alone. As they neared the heading Steve had raced ahead to greet the men they were relieving. A flicker of pain, maybe of weariness, crossed the father's face as he followed his son.

The work in the tunnel was constant. One gang stepped in and took the tools from the hands of the men working in the heading. Hour upon hour, shift after shift the ceaseless, constant war with the river went on. The muckers in Big Tim's gang seized the shovels while the handles were still warm and tore into the muck pile. The iron-gang clambered up the sides of the tube and finished the half-tightened bolts left by the men going out. There were a few words, a laugh, and thirty tired sandhogs straggled up the tunnel while Big Tim's men took over.

Here in the heading beneath the river was a mad world. The sandhogs, stripped to the waist, drenched with sweat, labored like fiends in the scorching heat. The roar of the air thundering in through the feed lines provided an ever-present bass against which the clang of the tools rang in counterpoint. The tunnel was a vapory hell in which steaming demons crouched. The ever changing pressure caused a fog that cast an opalescent veil about the gleaming lights. Figures became dim and hazy, then sprang into bold relief, only to fade again. The completed section of the tube stretched off into ghostly distance out of which roared the strings of muck cars. Weird gurglings arose from the bottom where streams of water oozed in against the pressure.

On a wooden platform suspended across the center of the tunnel worked the iron gang. Monstrous Negroes from Senegal and Jamaica swung their ponderous wrenches up and down in rhythmic motion as they tightened the curved iron plates. Through the vague, misty light of the heading, their bobbing figures weaved and swayed, casting grotesque shadows on the circular walls.

Below, on the tunnel floor labored the muckers, the infantry of the sandhogs. Their flying shovels heaped the greedy muck-cars high with spoil of the river bed.

At the forward end of the tunnel stood the shield. This huge steel cylinder fitted closely over the advancing section of the tube. It was braced vertically and horizontally. The single cross-member bisecting the shield formed a working platform. The upright webbing divided the upper and lower sections into pockets, of which there were six.

Around the rear circumference were eighteen hydraulic jacks. These pistons thrust against the last ring of segments of the completed tunnel lining. When pressure was applied they forced the shield ahead into the river bed.

Joe Redman and his son climbed the flanges of the iron and crawled into the upper center pocket. With them came Frank Webber, the third miner of the gang. Their helpers busied themselves gathering together the tools and bags of hay. Little was said as the miners advanced to the firing step of the tunnel. Here the threat of the river was greatest.

Before them the face of the tunnel trembled in a delicate balance. A wall of air billowed against the carefully placed boards that braced the heading. Outside, the river strove with its millions of tons of fluid death to pass the invisible barrier and flood the tunnel. Inside, beneath the sloping steel hood of the shield the miners stepped to the attack.

The quarters were cramped, the working platforms were but four feet wide. Steve crawled beneath a projecting brace and studied the face in the right pocket. To the left, Frank Webber, an old-timer from the mines of England, critically shifted a face-board. In the center pocket Joe Redman stripped the Khaki shirt from his shoulders and tightened his belt. He reached out a calloused hand and lifted a pinch of sand. Slowly he sifted it between his fingers. Bewilderment crowded the wrinkles tightly around his eyes. Again he dipped into the wet muck with his fingers and tested the feel of the sand.

"Y'know, I don't like the looks of this stuff." An uncertainty in the words stopped the labors of the others. "It's changed a lot since yesterday."

"What's bothering you, dad?" asked Steve.

"I'm not sure, kid. This stuff doesn't feel right. We've had good ground all the way across the river but it looks as though we've run into a glacial deposit."

"Gor-blime," laughed Webber. " 'E's started already. I might 'ave knowed. No sooner does young Steve put 'is foot inside the 'eadin' than Joe starts fussin'. The face is all right, Joe, it's you that's balmy."

"Maybe," said Joe. "But I've worked under this river before. I'm pretty sure we hit a stretch of gravel along about here on the last job. I wouldn't want to run into a wall of marbles with too many boards out of the face."

"Oh, don't be a crêpe-hanger," laughed Steve. "This face is fine. Look at it—it cuts like cheese."

He sliced a spoonful of muck from the wall before him. Streams of gray, fine-grained sand slithered in the wake of his shovel and cascaded into tiny mounds at his feet. An eerie whistling grew to a moan as the compressed air in the heading forced its way through the gap. Again the shovel cut deeply. The moan grew to a wail.

"Careful there," Joe said sharply. "You've got a river over your head and it would like to come in."

Steve laughed. His father was of the old school. Caution—care—precision—they were things for old men to worry about. Speed—that was the order of the day. Drive ahead, make tunnel, keep the shield moving—this was the way of the young sandhog.

The corded muscles of his back leaped beneath the sweat-drenched skin as he slashed at the wall. He swept the sand down past the working platform into the bottom where it piled about the legs of the muckers. Half turning, he grabbed a plank from the outstretched arms of his helper and fitted it against the face. Bracing it with his knee, he packed the edges with hay and reached for the screw-jack. This he swung into place and twisted the handles until a warning crack came from the plank.

"This face is all right, dad," he said. "We won't have any trouble with it."

He drove at his work. The moan of the air sang a wild tune in his ears. The surge of the pressure sent the blood pounding through his veins. This was his trade, a man's trade; fighting the river; driving a tunnel beneath the threatening flood; pitting his skill and his strength against the elements.

"Take it easy, young fellow," cautioned Joe. "That's a shovel you have there, not a broom. Get a few boards in the face before you take out any more sand."

"It'll hold," said Steve. "If I stop to put a board in now I'll lose time."

"Lose time—you'll lose your fool life if you don't," cried Joe. "Get some boards in there and pack them with hay, I tell you!"

"I say, Joe," called Webber from the far pocket, "stop blaggardin' the boy. 'E's a right fine miner."

"That's right, Frank," shouted Steve. "You tell him. He seems to think I'm still a kid."

He turned and with a swooping slice sheered clear to the edge of the hood. The air whined angrily through the exposed face. From the lower section of the pocket a low moan sounded like the cry of a beast in pain.

"You young fool!" cried Joe. "Have you no ears? Listen! Even the air is trying to tell you. Get some planks in there and close up that face. Damn the day I ever brought you into a tunnel."

Steve grinned. "Better get some work done in your own pocket or I'll have to come in and help you."

"Why—you—you young pup!" Joe lifted his shovel above his head as though to strike. A blazing flash of rage shook him. Slowly he lowered the shovel.

From the other pocket his son studied him. The grin faded a little.

"Nice temper you've got," he said. "I used to wonder what it was that kept you and mother apart. I think I can guess."

He bent to his work with renewed savagery. His shovel bit deep.

A tiny stream of sand ran from the cut. It slithered down onto the working platform. Quickly. It poured in ever increasing volume. Only then, Steve realized his mistake. He reached for a plank and jammed it upright against the flow.

"Dad!" he yelled. "It's sliding—it's going!"

A section of the face melted away like frost beneath a blow torch. The wail of the air rose, mad, strident. A myriad of screaming fiends were unleashed in the heading.

Stripped of its friendly mask of sand, the true nature of the face stood forth. Small round stones, rubbed smooth by the relentless surge of ancient ice packs, poured from the open face. They rained down about Steve's legs. The air clouded with a sudden mist. Rapid decompression was drenching the tunnel with fog.

"What have you done?" screamed Joe. "I told you—I told you—it's a blow—"

A blow! The constant dread of the tunnel man. When the surging air explodes upward through the broken face and bursts in a frothing geyser on the surface—when the sodden muck of the river bed pours into the heading—when the river, no longer held in check by the wall of air, rushes in to drown the sandhogs—that is a blow.

From the far pocket Webber took up the cry. "A blow! A blow!" It spread along the tunnel to the toiling sandhogs with lightning rapidity. "A blow! The face is gone!" Muckers dropped their shovels and plunged in headlong flight toward the bulkhead. The iron men cast aside their wrenches and joined in the mad panic. "A blow! A blow!" The cry echoed along the dank walls of the tunnel and sent men rushing for the locks. The air roared down the tube with a sudden violence. A blinding fog enveloped the heading. The lights dimmed. Terror struck at the struggling workers.

In the face, ahead of the shield stood the miners. Theirs was the fault and theirs the responsibility. Upon their shoulders rested the fate of the gang. If they stopped the mad rush of air even for a moment, lives would be saved. Others might race to the protection of the locks. They must stand and fight the blow to the last.

With a heaving lurch Joe leaped into the pocket beside his son. Tearing a plank from the hands of Webber, who had crossed to help him, he thrust it into the wound. There was a sudden sound of splintering wood and the plank shriveled and was sucked into the gaping hole. Into the growing vacuum Steve flung his shovel, a pick, more planks, bags of hay, everything he could grab. Webber thrashed about the pocket passing tools and boards to the battling pair.

Steadily the sand and gravel poured from the face. The opening grew—a whirlpool of muck into which was drawn everything within reach. The men worked like fiends, pouring the offerings of boards and hay into the consuming maw of the blow. The air shrilled in a wild scream.

"Get out, kid—get out—we can't stop it." The words came in gasps from the laboring father. "Run—run, I tell you—"

Webber cast one despairing glance at the broken, twisted face and scrambled through the pocket. He jumped from the center platform and splashed into the rapidly rising water. A cry of fear burst from his throat as the chill water swirled about his waist. Thrashing about in the white gloom he blindly fought his way up the tunnel.

"Steve—" the cry was wrenched from Joe's contorted lips as he forced a plank into the breach, "Steve, son— get out—go, I say—I can't hold it any longer."

"I—I—can't!" cried Steve.

Standing beside his father in the cramped confines of the narrow pocket the boy was trapped. All unconsciously the older man had constantly shifted his feet as he strove to check the blow. As the muck piled in he had fought his way up and up, keeping his legs free. Bewilderment, fright, the awful newness of a blow had held Steve to one place. Now the muck was piled high about his hips. He heaved backward, dragging at his legs. The muck held fast. He tore at the clinging pile fighting to free himself. It was useless. He was trapped.

"I'm licked, dad!" he screamed. "Get out—you go—"

The shrieking blast of the escaping air drowned out his words. Fog blinded him. He leaned against a brace. Be-

side him his father loomed a dark mass in the billowing
mist. Out of the mad inferno came his voice.

"A plank, kid. Hand me a plank—one chance—it's
jamming—"

The whirling mass had clogged. Some slight obstruc-
tion in the river bed had caused a momentary stoppage of
the blow. It must be blocked, crammed tightly with bags
of hay and planks before the driving air blasted a way
through. One plank, a single bag, anything would serve.
Steve thrust blindly with his hands. He strained to the utmost limit of his reach. Nothing but muck met his hands.

"A plank—a plank!" The despairing cry sounded like
the call of doom. Seconds were precious. Time was life
itself. A haggard face loomed suddenly beside him. Horrid realization shone from his father's eyes. The pockets
were bare. Not a bag nor a plank remained.

The wail of air was rising. The shrill cry of the tempest
as it spun into the gap rose higher and higher. Now—now
was the time to block it. A moment hence—thirty seconds—and it would be too late. The hole would widen
and the scant air remaining in the tunnel would burst
through. With the restraining pressure gone the river
would pour a deluge into the heading.

Steve tried to grin. He had worked a man's trade; he
wanted to die a man. A hand fell on his shoulder. A
straining face was pressed close to his.

"One chance, kid." The words were torn from lips
close to his ear. "One chance—tell her I sent her boy
home—tell her, if it works."

Steve clutched wildly at his father's naked shoulders as
the truth burned into his brain. His hands tore at the per-
spiration covered arms.

"Don't! Don't—!"

Joe wrenched—hurled himself away. He sprang at the
twisted hole in the face. The air caught him—lifted him
—smashing him into the breech in a horrible upward
leap. The swirling sand packed tightly about him. The
wail of the air lessened—it moaned dully—it stopped.

THE SECRET LIFE OF
WALTER MITTY

by James Thurber

"WE'RE GOING THROUGH!" The Commander's voice was like thin ice breaking. He wore his full-dress uniform, with the heavily braided white cap pulled down rakishly over one cold gray eye. "We can't make it sir. It's spoiling for a hurricane, if you ask me." "I'm not asking you, Lieutenant Berg," said the Commander. "Throw on the power lights! Rev her up to 8,500! We're going through!" The pounding of the cylinders increased; ta-pocketa-pocketa-pocketa-*pocketa-pocketa*. The Commander stared at the ice forming on the pilot window. He walked over and twisted a row of complicated dials. "Switch on No. 8 auxiliary!" he shouted. "Switch on No. 8 auxiliary!" repeated Lieutenant Berg. "Full strength in No. 3 turret!" shouted the Commander. "Full strength in No. 3 turret!" The crew, bending to their various tasks in the huge, hurtling eight-engined Navy hydroplane, looked at each other and grinned. "The Old Man'll get us through," they said to one another. "The Old Man ain't afraid of Hell!" . . .

"Not so fast! You're driving too fast!" said Mrs. Mitty. "What are you driving so fast for?"

"Hmm?" said Walter Mitty. He looked at his wife, in the seat beside him, with shocked astonishment. She seemed grossly unfamiliar, like a strange woman who had yelled at him in a crowd. "You were up to fifty-five," she

said. "You know I don't like to go more than forty. You
were up to fifty-five." Walter Mitty drove on toward Waterbury in silence, the roaring of the SN202 through the
worst storm in twenty years of Navy flying fading in the
remote, intimate airways of his mind. "You're tensed up
again," said Mrs. Mitty. "It's one of your days. I wish
you'd let Dr. Renshaw look you over."

Walter Mitty stopped the car in front of the building
where his wife went to have her hair done. "Remember to
get those overshoes while I'm having my hair done," she
said. "I don't need overshoes," said Mitty. She put her
mirror back into her bag. "We've been all through that,"
she said, getting out of the car. "You're not a young man
any longer." He raced the engine a little. "Why don't you
wear your gloves? Have you lost your gloves?" Walter
Mitty reached in a pocket and brought out the gloves. He
put them on, but after she had turned and gone into the
building and he had driven on to a red light, he took
them off again. "Pick it up, brother!" snapped a cop as the
light changed, and Mitty hastily pulled on his gloves and
lurched ahead. He drove around the streets aimlessly for
a time, and then he drove past the hospital on his way to
the parking lot.

. . . "It's the millionaire banker, Wellington McMillan,"
said the pretty nurse. "Yes?" said Walter Mitty, removing
his gloves slowly. "Who has the case?" "Dr. Renshaw
and Dr. Benbow, but there are two specialists here, Dr.
Remington from New York and Dr. Pritchard-Mitford
from London. He flew over." A door opened down a
long, cool corridor and Dr. Renshaw came out. He
looked distraught and haggard. "Hello, Mitty," he said.
"We're having the devil's own time with McMillan, the
millionaire banker and close personal friend of Roosevelt.
Obstreosis of the ductal tract. Tertiary. Wish you'd take a
look at him." "Glad to," said Mitty.

In the operating room there were whispered introduc-
tions: "Dr. Remington, Dr. Mitty. Dr. Pritchard-Mitford,
Dr. Mitty." "I've read your book on streptothricosis,"
said Pritchard-Mitford, shaking hands. "A brilliant per-
formance, sir." "Thank you," said Walter Mitty. "Didn't

know you were in the States, Mitty," grumbled Remington. "Coals to Newcastle, bringing Mitford and me up here for a tertiary." "You are very kind," said Mitty. A huge, complicated machine, connected to the operating table, with many tubes and wires, began at this moment to go pocketa-pocketa-pocketa. "The new anaesthetizer is giving away!" shouted an interne. "There is no one in the East who knows how to fix it!" "Quiet, man!" said Mitty, in a low, cool voice. He sprang to the machine, which was now going pocketa-pocketa-queep-pocketa-queep. He began fingering delicately a row of glistening dials. "Give me a fountain pen!" he snapped. Someone handed him a fountain pen. He pulled a faulty piston out of the machine and inserted the pen in its place. "That will hold for ten minutes," he said. "Get on with the operation." A nurse hurried over and whispered to Renshaw, and Mitty saw the man turn pale. "Coreopsis has set in," said Renshaw nervously. "If you would take over, Mitty?" Mitty looked at him and at the craven figure of Benbow, who drank, and at the grave, uncertain faces of the two great specialists. "If you wish," he said. They slipped a white gown on him; he adjusted a mask and drew on thin gloves; nurses handed him shining . . .

"Back it up, Mac! Look out for that Buick!" Walter Mitty jammed on the brakes. "Wrong lane, Mac," said the parking-lot attendant, looking at Mitty closely. "Gee. Yeh," muttered Mitty. He began cautiously to back out of the lane marked "Exit Only." "Leave her sit there," said the attendant. "I'll put her away." Mitty got out of the car. "Hey, bettter leave the key." "Oh," said Mitty, handing the man the ignition key. The attendant vaulted into the car, backed it up with insolent skill, and put it where it belonged.

They're so damn cocky, thought Walter Mitty, walking along Main Street; they think they know everything. Once he had tried to take his chains off, outside New Milford, and he had got them wound around the axles. A man had had to come out in a wrecking car and unwind them, a young, grinning garageman. Since then Mrs. Mitty always made him drive to a garage to have the chains taken off.

The next time, he thought, I'll wear my right arm in a sling; they won't grin at me then. I'll have my right arm in a sling and they'll see I couldn't possibly take the chains off myself. He kicked at the slush on the sidewalk. "Overshoes," he said to himself, and he began looking for a shoe store.

When he came out into the street again, with the overshoes in a box under his arm, Walter Mitty began to wonder what the other thing was his wife had told him to get. She had told him, twice before they set out from their house for Waterbury. In a way he hated these weekly trips to town—he was always getting something wrong. Kleenex, he thought, Squibb's, razor blades? No. Toothpaste, toothbrush, bicarbonate, carborundum, initiative and referendum? He gave it up. But she would remember it. "Where's the what's-its-name?" she would ask. "Don't tell me you forgot that what's-its-name." A newsboy went by shouting something about the Waterbury trial.

. . . "Perhaps this will refresh your memory." The District Attorney suddenly thrust a heavy automatic at the quiet figure on the witness stand. "Have you ever seen this before?" Walter Mitty took the gun and examined it expertly. "This is my Webley-Vickers 50.80," he said calmly. An excited buzz ran around the courtroom. The Judge rapped for order. "You are a crack shot with any sort of firearms, I believe?" said the District Attorney, insinuatingly. "Objection!" shouted Mitty's attorney. "We have shown that the defendant could not have fired the shot. We have shown that he wore his right arm in a sling on the night of the fourteenth of July." Walter Mitty raised his hand briefly and the bickering attorneys were stilled. "With any known make of gun," he said evenly, "I could have killed Gregory Fitzhurst at three hundred feet *with my left hand*." Pandemonium broke loose in the courtroom. A woman's scream rose above the bedlam and suddenly a lovely, dark-haired girl was in Walter Mitty's arms. The District Attorney struck at her savagely. Without rising from his chair, Mitty let the man have it on the point of the chin. "You miserable cur!" . . .

"Puppy biscuit," said Walter Mitty. He stopped walking and the buildings of Waterbury rose up out of the misty courtroom and surrounded him again. A woman who was passing laughed. "He said 'Puppy biscuit,' " she said to her companion. "That man said 'Puppy biscuit' to himself." Walter Mitty hurried on. He went into an A & P., not the first one he came to but a smaller one farther up the street. "I want some biscuit for small, young dogs," he said to the clerk. "Any special brand, sir?" The greatest pistol shot in the world thought a moment. "It says 'Puppies Bark for It' on the box," said Walter Mitty.

His wife would be through at the hairdresser's in fifteen minutes, Mitty saw in looking at his watch, unless they had trouble drying it; sometimes they had trouble drying it. She didn't like to get to the hotel first; she would want him to be there waiting for her as usual. He found a big leather chair in the lobby, facing a window, and he put the overshoes and the puppy biscuit on the floor beside it. He picked up an old copy of *Liberty* and sank down into the chair. "Can Germany Conquer the World Through the Air?" Walter Mitty looked at the pictures of bombing planes and of ruined streets.

. . ."The cannonading has got the wind up in young Raleigh, sir," said the sergeant. Captain Mitty looked up at him through tousled hair. "Get him to bed," he said wearily, "with the others. I'll fly alone." "But you can't, sir," said the sergeant anxiously. "It takes two men to handle that bomber and the Archies are pounding hell out of the air. Von Richtman's circus is between here and Saulier." "Somebody's got to get that ammunition dump," said Mitty. "I'm going over. Spot of brandy?" He poured a drink for the sergeant and one for himself. War thundered and whined around the dugout and battered at the door. There was a rending of wood and splinters flew through the room. "A bit of a near thing," said Captain Mitty carelessly. "The box barrage is closing in," said the sergeant. "We only live once, Sergeant," said Mitty, with his faint, fleeting smile. "Or do we?" He poured another brandy and tossed it off. "I never see a man could hold his brandy like you, sir," said the sergeant. "Begging your pardon, sir." Captain Mitty stood up and strapped on his huge Webley-Vickers automatic. "It's forty kilometres through hell, sir," said the sergeant. Mitty finished one last brandy. "After all," he said softly, "what isn't ?" The pounding of the cannon increased; there was the rat-tat-tatting of machine guns, and from somewhere came the menacing pocketa-pocketa-pocketa of the new flame-throwers. Walter Mitty walked to the door of the dugout humming "Auprès de Ma Blonde." He turned and waved to the sergeant. "Cheerio!" he said. . . .

Something struck his shoulder. "I've been looking all over this hotel for you," said Mrs. Mitty. "Why do you have to hide in this old chair? How did you expect me to find you?" "Things close in," said Walter Mitty vaguely. "What?" Mrs. Mitty said. "Did you get the what's-its-name? The puppy biscuit? What's in that box?" "Over-shoes," said Mitty. "Couldn't you have put them on in the store?" "I was thinking," said Walter Mitty. "Does it ever occur to you that I am sometimes thinking?" She looked at him. "I'm going to take your temperature when I get you home," she said.

They went out through the revolving doors that made a faintly derisive whistling sound when you pushed them. It was two blocks to the parking lot. At the drugstore on the corner she said, "Wait here for me. I forgot something. I won't be a minute." She was more than a minute. Walter Mitty lighted a cigarette. It began to rain, rain with sleet in it. He stood up against the wall of the drugstore, smoking . . . He put his shoulders back and his heels together. "To hell with the handkerchief," said Walter Mitty scornfully. He took one last drag on his cigarette and snapped it away. Then, with that faint, fleeting smile playing about his lips, he faced the firing squad; erect and motionless, proud and disdainful, Walter Mitty the Undefeated, in-scrutable to the last.

THE END